GARY M LEE

The Artificial Divide

A Journey to Save the Human Race from AI

To: Craig & Kerri

Hope you enjoy
this book.

Contents

1

The Europa Colony

As Sara floated in her room staring out of her window at the dark space surrounding the asteroid mining colony, she was contemplating her future. She could just make out Jupiter as the bright object in the sky which harbored a moon called Europa containing the home colony where she grew up. Her plan was to return to Europa when her work rotation on the asteroid was complete, but now she was learning things about herself and the fate of her colony that prompted her into action. She needed to try and find other human colonies she was convinced were out there, in order to help save the human species.

Growing up on Europa, Sara was a popular girl at her church school and bible study with her short dark hair and fit body. But instead of socializing with her friends after school, she spent much of her time alone in the school library trying to learn more about her family history and her place in the large human colony where she lived. Over time, she became increasingly frustrated in her efforts to learn more, given that the colony leadership controlled all the books and files she was able to access. When she was younger, she asked her parents about their family history, but they only could tell her that her ancestors had arrived hundreds of years ago and they had no recollection of any family history before the colony. This gave her the impression that the colony existed long before anyone could remember. She even asked some of her teachers in school, but the church elders who ran the colony were not tolerant of these types of questions and did not want the school curriculum to cover this part of their history.

Europa was a water world with deep oceans covered in ice, orbiting the large gas giant known as Jupiter. The colony was a large structure that was constructed well below the thick ice layer that covered the surface of Europa. Sara would sometimes explore the colony's many open areas, riding up and down the shiny escalators that allowed movement between levels. She was not allowed on the top level where the colony leaders lived and worked, nor was she allowed down on the lower levels where fusion reactors were used to power the colony and to split liquid water molecules into oxygen and hydrogen atoms. Just above these lower levels was a wide-open area containing acres of farmland providing food for the colony. The remaining levels contained homes for the workers along with shopping, schools and churches.

Sara's favorite place in the colony was the large central open area where multiple floors overlooked a large park containing grass and trees. Each colonist was assigned a job such as food production, teaching, medical services, colony maintenance or ministering. Sara's father worked in food production while her mother taught preschool, but Sara excelled in math and science and wanted to pursue that as a career. Her grandparents and aunts and uncles lived in apartments close to where her family lived making it easy for them to get together for holidays or religious celebrations. They all attended church together along with many other families that lived in their section of the colony.

A year before she graduated from school, Sara became friends with Adrian Nelson, one of the brightest people in her computer programming class. They both had a strong interest in programming and computer technology, and therefore gravitated to one and other. Sara also liked his no-nonsense personality, which sometimes irritated others. One day after class, they were sitting in a park outside of school.

"Do you ever wonder what's outside of these walls?" Sara asked as she pointed around her.

"I don't think the leaders want us to know anything besides what we need to know to keep the colony running," replied Adrian.

"Aren't you curious about what we are doing here?" inquired Sara.

"Well, it's clear that someone or something built this colony and our ancestors may have come from elsewhere, but you can't say that to anyone or you will be in trouble with the church. The church leaders say that God created this colony for us to live, work and worship in, and we should not question it," Adrian replied in a hushed tone.

"What about the robotic tanker ships that are constantly arriving to export hydrogen and oxygen from our colony?" Sara asked.

Adrian replied, "No one really knows what their purpose is and where they are headed, but the church leaders just tell us they are doing God's work and we shouldn't question things like that."

"But what do you think?" Sara pushed him for more of his

thoughts.

Adrian paused while he looked at her. "It doesn't matter what I think. I just want to be part of God's kingdom and do whatever I can to support the colony."

Sara had many more questions, but it was clear that Adrian didn't have the answer for them, or even thought about these things himself. She couldn't understand why others were not as curious as she was. They said their goodbyes and Sara headed home.

The colony was constructed at a time long before anyone could remember. It supported about 5000 humans in a large structure about 15 km below the icy surface of Europa which protected the population from the high amount of radiation that it's mother planet, Jupiter, produced. The colony was expansive and had spacious apartments for the inhabitants along with large open spaces with artificial sunlight. The colonists were happy to live, work and play in this environment as long as they abided by the church laws. Fusion reactors not only powered the colony, they also supplied the energy required to separate hydrogen and oxygen from the water below Europa's icy crust. The hydrogen was used by the colonist to power the fusion reactors and the oxygen provided breathable air, but they also produced enough to supply the large robotic tanker spaceships that arrived weekly. Pipelines from the colony up to the moon's surface fed these elements to the tankers with little involvement from the colonists unless repairs were needed.

Life in the colony was pleasant if not a little mundane. The fusion reactors provided all the energy they needed to create artificial sunlight and support the automated factories that provided food, medicine and other products that were needed by the colonists. The colonists had some freedom in selecting jobs based on their skill set, but the colony leadership could assign people to critical roles such as maintaining the colony infrastructure, as well as maintaining a healthy human population. The prime directive of the colony was to make sure there was a steady flow of hydrogen and oxygen to the arriving tanker ships per God's will. The colonists were taught not to question God's will.

All of the colonists were white, devote Christians and lived by the word of God. Their bible told them that God created the Europa colony for them and they should dedicate their lives to follow the word of God by supporting and maintaining the colony. People understood that they were on one of Jupiter's moons and near an asteroid belt, but generally didn't ponder or discuss what was outside of this domain without retribution from the church leadership and their enforcement division. Since the colony was deep within the ice, there was no way to leave the colony and even if a colonist wanted to make an attempt, there was no way for a human to survive on Europa's surface or in one of the robotic tanker ships.

Although there were no non-human animal species in the colony, there was a lot of greenery with fields and trees to make life more pleasant for the human population. The floor dedicated to farming contained a large number of fruit, vegetable and other plant species grown using hydroponics. On several occasions, Sara's father brought her down to the farming level where he worked, and she could spend hours exploring the aisles of greenery. She was fascinated by all of the different species of plants growing at the farm, and always had many questions for her father.

"Where did these trees and plants come from?" she asked him one day.

"They've been here for as long as anyone can remember," he replied. "We only need to keep them healthy since they provide all the food we need."

Exercise is one of the key elements of their life on Europa as they needed to maintain bones and muscles in the reduced gravity. Although they had no concept of living in a higher gravity environment, their religious teachings told them that regular exercise was a way to honor the body God had given them. Sara routinely jogged in one of the parks near her apartment where she lived with her brother and parents. The park was in the large open area below their apartment which made it easy for her to access it. She enjoyed this routine as it not only made her feel better, but also gave her time to think without other distractions. One day while jogging, she stopped to rest near a shade tree when she spotted a man who looked like he was hiding from someone behind a boulder.

"Are you OK?" She asked as she approached him.

As his eyes darted around, he said, "Are you with the church?"

"No, I'm a student," she replied, "why are you hiding here?"

"I'm an archivist from the church and uncovered something that the church doesn't want the colonist to know about," he said as they started to hear rapid footsteps coming closer. "Can I trust you?"

"With what?" she asked before he thrust a memory stick into her hand.

"Please keep this safe," he said as he got up to start running away from her.

Sara was confused, but tucked the memory stick in her shoe to hide it. Suddenly, two people from the church enforcement division came around the corner, grabbed the man and carried him away. Another church officer appeared and questioned Sara.

"Why were you here?" she asked Sara.

Sara explained that she was just taking a rest while jogging.

"Did he tell you anything or give you anything?" the officer asked.

Sara shook her head as she felt the memory stick rubbing against her foot in her shoe.

"Are you telling me the truth?" the officer got close to her face.

"Yes!" she replied in a stern voice.

The officer stared at her a moment longer before letting let her go and Sara was left a bit shaken up by the whole event. The colony was always a very peaceful place and she had never seen anyone arrested by the church enforcement division before. She questioned herself as to why she didn't turn over the memory stick to the officer, but decided that she wanted to see what it contained first. Since he was a church archivist, maybe it contained some of the colonies early history which she was always curious about. Her interest in her family history and the history of the colony outweighed her concern about retribution from the church.

The next day in class, she told Adrian what had happened and showed him the memory stick. He quickly grabbed it from her before anyone else in class saw what she was holding. It was illegal to own memory sticks or memory stick readers in the colony, but Adrian was as curious as she was and had an idea. His grandfather had an old storage locker near his house and he convinced her that they should go there after school. After descending an escalator to one of the lower floors of the colony, they came across aisles of storage lockers that the colonists could use. It was a large dark warehouse that Sara had not been in before since her family had never needed the extra storage space. The area was empty when Adrian motioned Sara to follow him down one of the aisles to a locker that looked like it hadn't been opened in years.

"Okay, what's so special about this storage locker?" Sara asked.

"You'll see," replied Adrian as he entered a number on the keypad lock and they went in.

After rummaging around piles of old equipment, he found what he was looking for.

"See this?" As he showed her what looked like an old computer screen. "If I can power this old thing up, we should be able to read the memory stick."

"But I thought those were illegal," Sara questioned.

"They are today, but my grandfather had this long before the law changed and they never confiscated it."

"Do you think it still works?" asked Sara.

"I hope so," replied Adrian. "I just need to plug it into a power source."

Adrian was able to power it up after finding an old electrical socket on the storage locker wall, and the old equipment came to life. They looked at each other, and Sara had a smile on her face. He inserted the memory stick into the side of the device and a few files showed up on the old dusty screen. Using the old keyboard, Adrian started examining the files to see if he could spot anything of interest.

"Look at this," he said. "It's an old document that talks about the construction of the colony and the founding of the church."

After studying it for a while, Adrian said. "It appears that this document claims that there are other human colonies out there and we're not alone."

"That must be why the man in the park was running from the

officers," Sara said. "He found some information that he was not allowed to know."

"I'm not sure we should know this either," Adrian told her. "I don't want to be imprisoned."

But just as they started to study more of the document, the old computer failed and they were not able to restart it. Worse yet, it looked like the computer overheated, destroying the memory stick. As much as Sara wanted to learn more about what they had read, Adrian said that he wanted to forget he ever saw it. They made a vow to keep this information to themselves, not wanting to be imprisoned by the church for blasphemy. But Sara could not get this out of her mind, that there may be other colonies like Europa out there. Maybe this is where the tankers were headed.

Sara continued to live with her parents and brother until she finished school and went on to attend technical college, where she graduated as an expert in computer programming and computer communication. Although the colony had no means of communication with the outside, they had internal systems that provided communications between the inhabitant's computers along with providing data including news, general information and religious doctrine. No personal cell phones or wireless devices were available as the leaders felt it reduced socialization within the colony. Communication networks were also used between the computers that controlled and maintained the colony infrastructure including the space port where the tankers arrived to load their cargo. After graduation, Sara became part of the computer network maintenance team and was given a small apartment of her own near her parent's place. She and her family continued to attend church services together and she also spent time volunteering to help the elderly at an assisted living home near where she lived, as part of her church duties.

Her workday usually consisted of traveling around the colony to debug and repair computer network problems that might come up. On many occasions, she would also be assigned to help solve network problems involving various infrastructure equipment that kept the colony running and also protected the lives of the colonists. She soon became friends with some of her co-workers and they would sometimes go out to dinner together after their shift was over. No alcohol or recreational drugs were allowed in the colony so the dinners were usually a tame affair, but she enjoyed socializing with with other people her age. During one such dinner, Sara struck up a conversation with one of her co-workers named Dave Johnson.

"Have any interesting service calls this week?" Asked Sara

"Not really," replied Dave, "but I did get to travel down to the lower levels to work on a network issue with the fusion reactors."

"What was that like?" Sara's interest was piqued.

"Well, I didn't get to stay down there for a detailed tour, but these massive energy producing machines are quite impressive," Dave said.

Sara felt comfortable enough to ask Dave, "Do you ever wonder how these machines were created or where they came from?"

Dave looked seriously at her, "What are you talking about? Our bible tells us that God provided these to us for our survival. We would be nothing without God's grace."

Sara realized that Dave was not one to question things like she was and decided to change the subject. It appeared that she was one of the few colonists that just didn't go along with what she was told to think by the church. She was convinced that there must be other colonies like hers out there somewhere, but she also knew that voicing these thoughts could land her in prison, so she decided to keep them to herself. She generally enjoyed her work although it could become monotonous sometimes.

One morning when she came into work, Sara's boss was there to greet her. She was wondering if Dave had told her supervisors about her questions, but was soon relieved that it was about something else. She was selected to be part of a team that needed to repair a communication module on a space port valve sensor. The space port was used by the hydrogen and oxygen tankers, but was on the surface of Europa which was about 15 km above the colony. She was told that they needed to use a high-speed service elevator to get up to the surface and make the repairs. Sara had heard about the space port, but never thought she would go up there. The leader of her team was a man in his late 50's name Cal Hansen, who had been on the network maintenance team for over 30 years.

As they walked over to the old service elevator, Sara asked Cal, "Have you ever done this type of work before?"

"No.", Cal replied, "but about ten years ago, one of my co-workers traveled up the elevator to the surface. He said the view was glorious up there."

"How do they know that this elevator is safe?" Sara looked worried.

"Well, it's used periodically by the asteroid mining teams. They use it to get to their transport craft," Cal said. "Because of that, it's well maintained."

Sara had learned about the asteroid mining colony in school. Just as the Europa colony was providing hydrogen and oxygen per God's will, the asteroid mining colony provided various precious metals and other materials to robotic ore ships. The space port where the robotic tankers arrived, was also used le Europa colonists who were assigned to work in the asteroid colony. Sara had not met anyone who worked on an asteroid mining team, but heard that they only pick people with the skills to maintain the automated mining operation.

Cal briefed the team, "We have a bit of a ride ahead of us up to the surface, but that will give us time to get into our space suits and do final safety checks. Also, the radiation is pretty intense on the surface, so we need to work quickly."

Sara felt both thrilled and apprehensive about traveling up to the surface. The thought of viewing something outside the colony for the first time overwhelmed any apprehension she may have had. They finally made it over to the elevator entrance which was in a remote service tunnel on one of the top floors in the colony. Cal was the only one entrusted with the code to enter the service elevator room and he soon guided the team over to the elevator. Sara was a bit unsure about getting in a high-speed elevator that she had never ridden before, but she grabbed the space suit they gave her and entered the elevator. The door closed and Sara, Cal and two other workers from her team started the 30-minute ride to the surface. The gradual increase in speed as the elevator accelerated up to the surface was barely noticeable. On the way up, they helped each other into their space suits which provided some protection from the surface radiation. They also tested the suits to make sure the oxygen, communication and helmet lights worked properly.

Once at the surface elevator room, the elevator door opened and they entered an air lock, where they once more tested their suits before going out on the surface. Once the external airlock door opened and they stepped out onto the icy surface of Europa, Sara was mesmerized by what she saw. There was Jupiter's magnificent large orb hanging overhead. The vivid stripes of

12

clouds across the planet made her gasp. She was also amazed by the black space around her filled with stars. Across Europa's horizon, she saw spectacular water geysers in the distance shooting up into the black void. She could hardly hold in her excitement.

Cal saw her staring and said, "Sara! We need to keep moving as we don't have much time."

"I never knew this is what it was like on the surface," Sara said.

"I have heard about this from some of my friends who had worked on an asteroid mining team, but God doesn't want us living up here so he poisons the surface with a high amount of radiation," Cal replied.

After they walked further from the airlock, they started walking across the icy surface aided by spikes on their boots. Soon they were at the space port which was normally maintained by a few autonomous drones. There were landing pads consisting of large round platforms where the tankers land and dock with the filling pipes that originate down below on the lower floors of the colony. The drones make sure the pads are clear of ice and are controlled by sensors spread around the pads. There were four landing pads where the tankers land before filling with their cargo and then launch again in the low Europa gravity.

One of the flow rate sensors on a filling pipe had lost communication with the colony below, and their job was to replace a communication module quickly before they received too high of a radiation dose. After replacing and testing the module, they started to quickly walk back to the airlock before their radiation dose was too high. When they were getting close to the airlock, one of the workers slipped and fell into an ice crevice that suddenly opened up along their path. The rumbling ice quake knocked Sara to the ground, but she quickly got to her feet and rushed over to help but was grabbed by Cal before she too fell in. The worker was hanging on to an ice ledge 10 meters below the surface, but soon lost his grip and fell down into the deep chasm below. The remaining three team members stood there in horror as they heard his yelling stop on their voice channel.

"We need to help him!" Sara pleaded.

"There is nothing we can do now, it's the will of God," Cal said as he held her by her shoulders with a look of distress on his face.

"I don't think God would want people to die!" replied Sara.

"Think of it that he died helping the other people in the colony," Cal tried to reassure her even though he was also visibly upset. "His family will be sad but also proud of the sacrifice he made for our colony. Now quickly into the airlock before we receive too much radiation."

After re-entering the elevator room through the airlock, they joined each other in the elevator and took off their space suits during the 30-minute ride back down to the colony. They looked at each other as they thought about the loss of their colleague, but uttered no words. This experience had a profound effect on Sara, and she sat quietly in the elevator while pondering her future. Would she spend the rest of her life working on network problems, or is there something bigger in life, possibly beyond the colony. Maybe there are other colonies like Europa out there. After a few more months putting in her time at work, she was notified that there was an opening for a network technician on the asteroid mining operation that the colony also supported. Although this would take her away from her family for months at a time, it would allow her to experience things beyond what the colony could offer her.

2

Asteroid Technician

Sara was excited about starting a new job as an asteroid mining maintenance technician, but her family didn't seem to be happy about it. Women her age were expected to get married and have children as dictated by church doctrine. But Sara had proven her superior computer networking skills which were sorely needed after one of the senior mining technicians had recently retired. Because of this, the church leadership allowed her to peruse this new role. Before she was scheduled to start her new job, she met up with Adrian at the local park.

"What will your job be at the mining colony?" Adrian inquired.

"Maintaining the communication networks within the mining colony," Sara replied. "I'll also work to help maintain all the network communication with the mining equipment. They use autonomous mining robots which extract and gather the ore and move the material to ore ships which are much like the hydrogen and oxygen ships that we supply on Europa. It should be interesting but I will need to come up to speed quickly on all of the unique computer and communication equipment they use in the asteroid colony."

"Do you think the ore ships are headed to the same destination as the tanker ships?" he asked

"I don't know the answer to that question, but I do wonder if there are other colonies like Europa out there," she replied.

"We'll probably never know," Adrian said as he decided to change the subject.

"I bet you'll get home sick very quickly," He teased.

"Well, I certainly won't miss you!" She joked. "But seriously, I can still do God's work on the asteroid and I look forward to the new experience. My work here has gotten a bit monotonous lately."

"Will, now your work may go from monotonous to danger-ous," Adrian said. "I hear that some workers never return."

"I won't be one of those," she said. "I'm a very careful person."

Sara had the impression that if she stayed working on Europa, she would be expected into marrying someone like Adrian, but she had no desire to have a family, at least not at this point in her life. She learned that her parents' marriage was arranged by the church, and although they were kind to one and other, she always felt there was not a deep love between them. Maybe this was another reason she took the mining job, so she could at least delay having the church dictate what the rest of her life would look like. Although she really liked Adrian as a friend, she felt no romantic love for him, and she wondered if she was even capable of loving a man and having a family.

Before she left, Sara was required to take a physical exam along with an intensive training and safety class. This was dangerous work, and they needed to make sure the workers were up to the task. The asteroid was being mined due to the high density of precious metals and other valuable material that was near its surface. The material was extracted by robotic mining machines that were serviced and maintained by the mining team. There were about eighty Europeans that make up the mining team including doctors, cooks, mechanical and electrical technicians. There was also a director of mining operation along with his support staff that included a pastor who held periodic church services. Since there was no significant gravity on the asteroid, the work and living conditions were in a weightless environment. Because of this, the mining teams served six months on the asteroid and six months back on Europa in order to maintain healthy bodies.

The mining colony was like a miniature version of the Europa colony, but on an asteroid that was about two kilometers in diameter. The living quarters, control room and repair bays were all inside one structure on the side of the asteroid that faced Europa. Because the colony was on the dark side of the asteroid, there were powerful lights illuminating the mining operation next to the colony. On top of the colony structure, there was a large docking port that incoming shuttle craft could attach to when new crews arrived. There was a large service tunnel through the center of the asteroid that used conveyor tubes to take the ore from the colony side of the asteroid where the robotic miners operated, to the opposite side where the ore ships docked. The mine workers were not allowed in this tunnel or on the opposite side near the ore ship docking port unless a repair was needed that could not be completed using autonomous drones, but no one could remember the last time that was required. All of the mining was done near the colony as the robotic mining equipment was in frequent need of repair by the colonist in one of the colony service bays. One of the network maintenance teams jobs was to make sure there were no communication problems between the robotic mining equipment.

Being a new member of the mining staff, Sara was required to take several training classes before departure. During one of her training classes, someone asked, "Where did all of this come from?"

The instructor, somewhat annoyed by the question replied, "Just like our colony here on Europa, God provided everything we need to live and work. All he asks is that we live in peace, maintain the colonies and provide his tankers and ore ships with the materials he needs. In our bible, God tells us not to question the work we do at our home on Europa or the asteroid mining colony. He provides the living quarters, tools and shuttle craft that allows us to serve his needs."

Sara secretly wondered if the ore ships, like the hydrogen and oxygen tankers from Europa are actually headed to another human colony somewhere, like the ones that were mentioned in the documents on the memory stick she and Adrian had discovered. All she knew about the solar system was Europa, Jupiter and the asteroid she'd be working on. She wondered if there were other Europa's and asteroids out there, but she was smart enough to keep these questions to herself in order not to lose her job. The church served out harsh punishment for anyone who questioned what was said in their bible.

About a week after her training class was complete, she said goodbye to her family and to Adrian before walking with a large backpack containing her belongings over to the high-speed surface elevator that she used previously with the space port repair team. This time she was less apprehensive and knew what to expect on the ride to the surface. Unlike the large tanker craft which land on the surface of Europa, the crew shuttle craft landed directly on the structure above the elevator room and airlock. No spacesuits were required as they climbed a ladder and took a seat in the shuttle craft. The shuttle was used to replace about 40 of the miners who worked on a staggered shift for six months while 40 other miners who had about three months left on their shift remained on the asteroid.

The shuttle craft was a rectangular looking box with several engines on the outside to help it push away from Europa's weak gravity before traveling at a higher speed toward the asteroid colony. One half of the craft contained the crew quarters and rows of seats used during launch. The other half of the craft contained a large cargo area that was being filled with food and water along with other equipment needed by the mining team. During loading, the shuttle remained horizontal before being tipped up for launch. Sara found a seat next to another woman, who she found to be very attractive, named Rachel Dire. Rachel had long blonde hair that she normally kept in a bun on top of her head. Sara thought she looked like her aunt whom she had a warm relationship with.

"Have you taken this trip before?" Inquired Sara.

"This is actually my fifth trip to the Asteroid. I'm Rachel," she said.

"Hi, I'm Sara and this is my first time. I just joined as a networking specialist."

"That's quite a critical job," Rachel said. "I work with the lead doctor to maintain the health of people in the mining colony."

"That's also quite important," replied Sara.

Sara didn't understand why she felt so drawn to Rachel, but was quickly distracted when they were rotated back into their seats and the shuttle engines roared to life. The takeoff was smooth but there were no windows near her seat so she felt robbed of the amazing view of Jupiter that she saw on her repair mission. For the first time in her life, Sara felt the weightlessness of space which took her some time to get used to. But within a few days she mastered floating through the shuttle craft using the hand and footholds spread around the interior. She knew that she wouldn't feel the pull of gravity again for another 6 months and needed to get use to this new environment. The craft had small private quarters for each of the 40 passengers along with a large social area where they could also dine, along with a small chapel to hold church services. Sara spent her private hours reading, sleeping or sending messages to her family. But she also spent a lot of the two-week trip attending church services and socializing with others including Rachel.

Like Sara, Rachel's parents had a marriage arranged by the church, but unlike Sara's parents, they were truly in love with each other. Rachel grew up in a different section of the Europa colony, so she and Sara never crossed paths. Rachel had a natural ability to care for and nurture other people which drew her into the nursing profession. Maybe this is why Sara was so attracted to her. But Rachel was also very religious person who read the bible every day. She felt that God wanted her to join the mining colony as a nurturer and protector on the people who do the most dangerous work of repairing mining equipment. It appeared that she had no interest in a romantic relationship with another person. She even told Sara that her spouse was her work.

After two weeks of travel, they approached the asteroid shuttle port and were forced back in their seats as engines were fired to slow their speed. With no windows to see what was happening, they were told what to expect during docking.

Some small maneuvering engines controlled their orientation until they eventually heard the thud of the docking mechanism. The passengers departed the ship, and after the cargo was unloaded, another 40 souls boarded the ship for the trip back to Europa. Sara was assigned a small one room apartment and soon unpacked her belongings. Before long, her new supervisor named Janice Smith arrived at her room.

"Hi, my name is Janice and I will be your supervisor for the next three months which is when my replacement arrives. I hear that this is your first time at the asteroid colony, correct?"

"Yes, I just joined as a new network technician," Sara replied.

"I brought you your work uniform and would like to give you a tour of the facility if you are ready," Janice said.

"That would be great," Sara said. "Let me just put this uniform in my closet."

Sara followed Janice around the colony as she pointed out the cafeteria, recreational and social areas, and the chapel. Given that the asteroid had almost zero gravity, they traveled around using hand holds or simply pushed off the walls to float straight down hallways. Soon they arrived at what looked like a computer lab.

"This is where you will work," as Janice pointed to a work station. "I assume since you have had the training, I don't need to explain the details to you. You and other people on your team will be responsible for maintaining all of the communication equipment within our habitat, but more importantly, communication between all of the mining equipment. Your team works in three shifts of 8 hours each, giving you 16 hours off between your shifts. My office is just down this hall if you need anything. Any questions?"

Sara said no as Janice floated back to her office, and she was glad to see that her workstation looked almost identical to the one she trained on back on Europa. Soon another person arrived at the workstation next to Sara's.

"Hi, I'm Tom Hastings." Sara recognized him from the shuttle trip.

"Yes, we met on the shuttle," Sara replied.

"Looks like we are working the same shift together," Tom said. "I hear that you're a rookie. I can show you the ropes as this is my third trip to the mining colony."

"That would be great," Sara said with a smile. "Look forward to working with you."

Sara soon fell into a daily routine and started to enjoy her work. Most of her time was spent monitoring the health of the communications equipment throughout the colony and providing repair services when needed. She learned a lot from Tom as they worked together repairing networking gear and other equipment within the colony. It took her a while to get used to working in a weightless environment, but before long, anchoring herself using footholds became second nature. But after only a few weeks into her new job, an event occurred that shook Sara to her core.

A work order had come in to repair the network module on one of the mining robots which was no longer accepting commands from central control. Sara and Tom were assigned to this job and were soon putting on their space suits inside the airlock. This was the first time Sara had to do repair work outside the colony, but she was familiar with operating in a space suit.

"Have you done any work like this before?" asked Tom.

"I once helped repair a flow sensor on the surface of Europa," she replied. "It was at the tanker ship port."

"This is a bit different. Since we have no gravity, we need to maneuver outside using these thrusters on our space suits," as he pointed to some nozzles in the space suit backpack. "You should have learned about this in your training. Once we get to the robotic miner, we can attach ourselves while we work. Ready to go?"

She acknowledged him as they entered the airlock and were soon floating off to the side of the colony structure above the surface of the asteroid. From there, Sara could see one side of the habitat which looked like a smooth metal structure planted firmly in the side of the asteroid illuminated with artificial light. Down below them, she could see the large service bay openings where the robotic miners where repaired.

"Try out your thrusters," Tom said through the comms system.

At first, she pressed the controller too long and started to float away from the surface. Tom laughed at her but followed her path. After some practice and help from Tom, she learned how to control her movements, and she and Tom worked their way over to the disabled mining robot which was only about 200 meters from the habitat. The robot was a large cube about five meters on a side. It had four legs that it uses to attach to the surface with augers, and a large central auger drill that extracted the minerals. The minerals were then transferred through a long conveyor pipe that attached to the robot miner on one end and ran through the central tunnel to the ore ships waiting on the other side of the asteroid.

After they floated over to the miner, they attached themselves with straps next to the service bay. Tom opened the bay door and located and removed the defective network module. Sara handed him the replacement module which he plugged into the empty slot. Suddenly, the miner came to life and started vibrating wildly just as Tom was closing the service door, and the auger drill started up again. Someone must have failed to send a disable command to the miner so it started operating after the communication module booted up.

Their straps were still attached to the miner and caused them to start shaking violently.

"Quick, release your strap!" Tom yelled. "There must have been a glitch in the control system!"

They both released their straps and started floating away from each other. Sara was heading away from the surface while Tom started heading close to the auger drill which was extracting more material. Sara used her thrusters to maneuver back toward Tom while he tumbled dangerously close to the auger drill. Tom quickly controlled his thrusters to stop his tumbling and started moving away from the active miner. Suddenly, a small piece of ore broke away from the auger suction control and pierced Tom's spacesuit. He yelled for help as the impact had started him tumbling again away from the surface. Sara used her thrusters to maneuver towards Tom and stop his rotations. She could see the damage to his space suit and also the damage to his leg. It looked like the ore had pierced his lower right leg and she could see large droplets of blood in the zero-gravity environment. She grabbed the repair tape from his backpack and started to tape the damaged spacesuit, but it was too late. As she held onto him, she realized that his life was draining from his body. All she could do was yell "no!" as he died in her arms.

3

The Message

Sara used her thrusters to maneuver herself and Tom's body back to the habitat airlock. She had been around death before back on Europa, but this was different. She had little interaction with the technician who fell into the ice crevasse, unlike Tom, who she had been working with closely for a while now, so his death hit her hard. Rachel and the lead doctor met Sara at the airlock, but quickly realized that there was nothing they could do.

"Are you okay?" Rachel asked Sara while she started to remove her spacesuit.

Sara just stared ahead and slowly nodded as she watched the doctor float Tom's body out of the airlock and down the hallway towards the medical room.

"Let's get you out of this spacesuit and back to your quarters," Rachel insisted. "The director will want to speak to you about what happened, but I can put him off until you've had a chance to rest. Let's pray now for Tom"

Sara was not feeling very religious at that moment and wondered why God could let someone who was a good person like

Tom die like this. Rachel escorted Sara back to her room and gave her some sleeping pills to help her relax, but Sara couldn't shut her mind off. What if she had died out there like Tom? What has she accomplished with her life? She knew that her parents and brother loved her, but she had no interest in a relationship with another man and had no desire to get married. Although she had friends like Adrian and Tom in her life, she never thought of them in a romantic way. She wondered if something was wrong with her. Her religion said that everyone should get married to help populate the Europa colony, but she had no desire and was too independent to just get married to satisfy the religious leaders. Before long the sleeping pills started kicking in, and she drifted off to sleep floating in her room.

The next morning Rachel knocked on Sara's door to see how she was doing. She had to knock a few times before Sara responded, and Sara was still a little groggy when she opened the door to see Rachel there. She was immediately struck by how beautiful Rachel looked this morning with her hair floating in a pony tail. Sara started to question herself on why she felt more attracted to Rachel instead of other men she was around. Maybe it was due to the trauma she had just been through with the death of Tom. She shook off these thoughts as Rachel drifted into her room.

"Good morning sleepy head. Did those pills work?" Rachel asked.

"I think so, but it's hard to wake up this morning," Sara replied.

"The director has a few questions about what happened out there. Can you meet him in his office in about an hour?"

Sara looked concerned. "What does he want to know? We did everything as we were trained."

"I wouldn't worry about it. He's just doing his job to make sure we all have a safe place to work," Rachel tried to reassure her.

"He needs to find out who failed to disable the mining robot command queue while we were replacing the network module," Sara looked angry. "That's what killed Tom!"

"Now calm down Sara," Rachel said in a reassuring voice. "I'm sure we will get all the answers shortly."

After Rachel left, Sara cleaned herself up and ate some breakfast. An hour later, Sara was in the director's office answering his questions. Rachel sensed that Sara was nervous about this meeting, so she came along for support. The director had the largest office in the habitat which was also one of the few offices with windows overlooking the mining operations. From two of the windows in his office he could observe and monitor some of the robotic mining equipment operating on the surface of the asteroid. Sara wondered if he was watching them when Tom was killed. Two additional windows overlooked the service bays where the miners were housed when they needed a major overhaul every four months or so. Under the external facing windows was his workstation and footholds where he spent a lot of his time, and on the opposite side of the office was a place for people to hold meetings.

After introductions, the director started the discussion. "Sara, I'm glad you're OK, and be reassured that Tom is with God in heaven now. He will be sorely missed and I've sent condolences to his family back on Europa. What caused the miner to start up just as you replaced the network module?"

"It's hard to say, but I think its command queue wasn't cleared properly when it first lost communications with us," Sara said with some anger in her voice. "Normally, when communication is lost, the miner is supposed to clear all of its action commands, but that didn't happen this time. We need to find out who was responsible."

"We will open an investigation," the director tried to reassure her. "So how do we prevent this in the future?"

"We should change our procedures to confirm that the command queue is cleared before communication modules are replaced. Someone should have verified this before we went out there," Sara argued.

"I will make sure we do a thorough investigation." After a pause he continued, "You seem to be one of the sharper ones on the comms team. I have a recurring problem that my team can't seem to solve. Can I ask you to lead an effort to improve our communication link with Europa? Some of their messages are not being received correctly."

"I can have a look at it," Sara said.

"Great! I will speak with your supervisor, and I'll let you know what we find out about the accident," the director said as he wrapped up the meeting.

Sara wasn't convinced that she would get an answer about Tom's death, but wanted to prove her capabilities to the director. Although Janice's team was now shorthanded with the death of Tom, the director convinced her that his communications problem needed some priority. Janice agreed as long as Sara worked on it when other higher priority tasks were not looming. Sara told her that she was fine doing some overtime work, since she didn't have a lot of things to do in her off hours. This would also help keep her mind off other worries in her life, which she tended to focus on during her idle time.

Janice decided to introduce Sara to a woman named Brenda Slator who was a habitat maintenance technician and had been working in the asteroid colony for many years. Brenda had a vast knowledge of the colony architecture and structure, so Janice took Sara to meet Brenda at her workstation and asked Brenda to tell Sara what she knew.

"Many years ago, I was told about some equipment used to communicate with Europa that was part of the colony when it was created by God," Brenda said. "No one can remember the last time we needed to do any maintenance work on it. In fact, I'm not even sure where it is."

"Brenda knows this habitat inside and out." Janice said as she left to go back to her office. "She should be able to help you find it."

"Nice to meet you, Brenda," Sara introduced herself. "I think I might know the best place to start".

Brenda and Sara moved to the director's office and started examining the monitor he used to communicate with Europa. It was an old-style screen on the wall next to a small keypad. Sara was amazed by how old the technology was compared to the latest equipment produced in the Europa factories. Sara examined the monitor and keypad, and could not find any means to remove it from the wall. The keypad was hard wired into a unique wall port through a metal encased cable, but that's all they could determine.

"Do you know where this port is connected to in another part of the habitat?" Sara asked.

"No, but I've seen a similar wall port in one of the storage rooms," said Brenda

"Let's check it out," Sara said as they headed out of the office.

Once in the storage room, they moved some old equipment to expose the wall port that Brenda had seen before.

"Are you sure this is connected to the port in the director's office?" asked Sara.

"I know of only two ports like this in the entire habitat and we now have seen both of them," replied Brenda. "Besides, his office is just down the hall and shares the same exterior wall, so they may be connected."

A cable came out from the side of the port and went up the wall and through the ceiling.

"Where does that go?" asked Sara.

"The only place that can lead to is outside the habitat," Brenda replied. "There are no other rooms above us."

"Looks like we need to go up on the roof. Are you spacewalk certified?" Sara asked Brenda.

"No, sorry. I decided not to re-certify since all my work is now inside the habitat."

"Well, I can go out and trace this cable. Where's the nearest airlock?" Sara inquired.

Brenda showed her the closest airlock and soon Sara was once again getting into a spacesuit. She thought of the dangers that she and Tom encountered on their last excursion, but convinced herself that this was less dangerous. For this spacewalk, she would stay close to the habitat and there was no mining equipment involved. Once she exited the airlock, Brenda kept track of her position using a location monitoring device attached to Sara's backpack. Brenda could track and communicate with Sara and guide her to the point where the cable exited the habitat. Once Brenda was back in the storage room, she guided Sara to the correct location.

"A little further to your right," Brenda guided her. "OK, you should be getting close now. There, do you see it?"

"Yes, I see it. It looks like the cable continues along the exterior. I will find out where it's going," Sara replied.

Sara used her spacesuit thrusters to follow the cable. It was hard to spot unless you knew what you were looking for, as it was partially hidden by the ridges of the habitat roof and dust from the mining operation. Soon she traced it to the edge of the habitat and saw that it traveled some distance across the asteroid surface.

"Did you find out where it's going?" Asked Brenda through the comms system.

"Yes, but it leads away from the habitat across the surface," Sara was breathing a little heavier now.

"I think you should come back in. The asteroid surface can be a dangerous place!" implored Brenda.

"No, I think I'll go a little further," Sara said. "I think I can see where it's going."

She traced the cable to a spot about 100 meters from the habitat. The cable stopped at a round dish that was about five meters in diameter and facing, where Sara thought, must be Europa. The dish was away from the illuminated part of the habitat, so she needed to turn on her helmet lights. She had enough air left to investigate the dish to see if she could see any problems with it. One thing that she found that could be reducing the signal strength was that it was covered with a layer of dust, probably kicked up from the mining operations. Although there was very little gravity on the asteroid, there was enough to keep the metallic dust settled on the dish, reducing its effectiveness. The dust came off easily as she brushed it with her glove, and it floated away from the dish. When she was almost done cleaning, she uncovered a small metal plate attached to the side of the dish with some writing on it. It said "Manufactured by Deep Space Dish Corporation, Houston Texas, Earth, 2052". She spent some time looking around for other information on the dish, but that was the only thing she found.

When she got back to the airlock and removed her spacesuit, she told Brenda about the communication dish that was covered in dust. After telling her that she may have fixed the problem by simply cleaning off the dish, she also told her about the plate.

"What do you think this means?" she asked. "Have you ever heard of a company called Deep Space Dish Corporation on Europa? What do you think the number means?"

"I don't know that company," Brenda replied. "But my grandfather used to tell us about dreams he had about a planet called Earth. We just thought it was the imagination of an old man."

They had no idea about the number next to the name as the Europa colony counted years differently.

"We were taught that Jupiter was our mother planet and the only one in the universe," Sara said. "Look at all the stars that we see in the sky. Do you think there are other colonies like Europa out there?"

"There could be, but the church will put you in prison if you mention any of this type of speculation. I don't want to hear any more about it," Brenda said as she floated back to her workstation.

Sara stayed there for a while taking it all in. She was now more convinced that there were other colonies out there beside Europa. Maybe Huston, Texas was another colony like Europa, but she had no concept of where it could be. To find out more, she decided to investigate the box on the wall of the storage room that was connected to the dish, but without Brenda's help. She told Janice that she needed to do more work on the box in order to improve Europa communications for the director. Of course, she had no idea what the box did, so after her normal shift, she took her tool belt to the storage room and started examining the box. It was almost like an ancient artifact that hadn't been opened in hundreds of years, maybe back when the colony was first created.

She found a tool she could use to open the box and after some effort was able to remove the lid. Inside, she could see that there were two communication modules, one connected to the cable that led to the director's keypad and one that was left disconnected. Since it was evening and most people were in their rooms sleeping, Sara decided to try something. She swapped the cable by connecting it to the unused module and then made her way over to the directors' office. Since no one was around, she slipped in and floated over to the keypad and monitor on his wall. It appeared that this module was not communicating with Europa, but with some other location. Maybe this module was used by whoever constructed the habitat.

The monitor was now full of messages and symbols in a format she had never seen before. She could see what almost looked like orders and directives being transmitted from somewhere and she was able to use the keypad to freeze the screen and scroll back through the incoming messages. She spent the next several hours reading through messages that had recently come in when one caught her attention. It read:

"Human replacement android manufacturing is moving forward as planned. Should be able to start phasing out human work colonies within the next Earth year."

This message raised many questions in her mind. Who sent this? What are androids? Where is Earth? But more chilling was the fact that someone or something was planning to "phase out human work colonies". Did that mean kill the humans and replace them with what they called androids? Her faith in God told her that this could not be true. But her religion never mentioned Earth or other work colonies. Sara decided to keep this information to herself as disclosing it may land her in a psychiatric ward or in prison. She went back to the storage room, swapped the modules back, closed the box and told Janice that repairs for the director were completed. Part of her wanted to forget what she had just read.

Sara tried to resume a normal life in the mining colony, but her new found knowledge kept her up at night. Are there other human colonies out there? Is she the only one in her colony who knows of the plan to replace humans? Does that mean kill off the humans in the Europa colony? She knew that she could not trust anyone else with this information and she knew that she could not warn the Europa colony. They would think she was crazy and going against God's word. Maybe she could confide in Adrian once her six-month shift on the asteroid was complete. But even he might think she was crazy. Sara decided to bide her time and search for other clues.

Sara became friends with Rachel after Tom's death. They spent some time together during their off hours and even went to church together in the small chapel. Rachel mentioned that she was once married, but her husband died in an accident in one of the Europa factories. Sara didn't understand why she felt so attracted to another woman, and tried to control her feelings, but Rachel made it hard for her, given their close friendship and her beauty. One evening they were alone in Rachel's apartment floating next to each other watching a video.

"Do you ever think about getting married again?" Sara asked.

"After my husband died, I decided that I won't marry anyone else. He was my one true love in life," Rachel replied. "How about you?"

"I haven't found the right person yet. I think I need the male version of you," Sara joked.

"I think you would find me too hard to live with," Rachel said with a sly smile.

Sara was sitting close, looking in Rachel's eyes when suddenly something took over her emotions and she kissed Rachel on the lips.

Rachel recoiled and said, "Sorry, I'm not attracted to you in that way. Besides, the Church could imprison you for acting like that."

"I'm sorry. I'm not sure what came over me. It won't happen again," apologized Sara. "I think I should go back to my apartment and get some rest before the long work day tomorrow."

Before Sara left, Rachel grabbed her hand. "God will find the right man for you. You just need to be patient."

It was at that point that Sara realized that she would never be happy in a traditional marriage as dictated by the church. She also realized there would be no relationship with Rachel in her future despite the strong attraction she felt towards her. As she floated down the hallway toward her quarters, a deep sadness came over her. When she got to her apartment, she tried to sleep, but was kept awake wondering if she was the only human who knew of a plan to replace human colonies with androids. She also started to realize that there is no happy life waiting for her back on Europa and the only person she felt sexually attracted to just rejected her. She was now convinced that there were other colonies like hers out there. Maybe one of them could provide her with a better life or at least a better purpose for her life. It was time for her to re-evaluate her future plans.

4

The Escape

Sara's enthusiasm for work started to spiral downward over the next several weeks. Rachel was acting cold and avoided being alone in the same room with her. She realized that once back in Europa, her family would start putting pressure on her to get married to a man she would never be sexually attracted to. But the main thing that kept her up at night was the knowledge that she possessed about the potential end of the human race. Unfortunately, she could not save the message from the director's communication screen and had no hard evidence of its existence. Without that, she could land in an institution back on Europa in the likely event they didn't believe her.

She now felt that she had two choices; keep quiet and live a miserable life back on Europa or find a way to leave. She started to ponder a radical idea of becoming a stowaway on one of the ore ships that she guessed were headed to other human colonies. Maybe by traveling to another colony, she could find out where the message she read on the director's monitor came from. Maybe she could warn other human colonies about what she had read in the message. This could lead her into danger, but no matter the outcome, anything would be better than her current life situation.

First, she had to learn more about these ore ships and decided to ask Brenda to meet her for lunch in the common area near her apartment.

"Hi Brenda, thanks for meeting me," greeted Sara.

Brenda looked a bit concerned. "I hope you don't want to discuss that message you found. It could easily be a fake message and goes against our church doctrine."

"Don't worry," Sara said. "I wanted to discuss something else. My job requires me to understand all of the communication equipment on this asteroid and you seem to have the most knowledge about the habitat."

"Happy to help," replied Brenda as she looked more relaxed.

Sara started asking a variety of questions related to the habitat, including the location of various types of equipment that may require communication modules. Then she turned to questions about the exterior.

"Do you know anything about the exterior equipment?" asked Sara.

"Not much. All of the exterior equipment such as the robotic miners are maintained by the mechanical team. I don't get involved in that," replied Brenda

"How about the ore conveyor system that transports the ore through the asteroid to the ore ships on the other side?" asked Sara.

"That tunnel through the asteroid has been there as long as anyone can remember," replied Brenda. "My understanding is that all of the equipment on the other side is maintained by autonomous drones. But when I just started working here many years ago, one of the old timers told me about a repair his team made on one of the tubes feeding the ore ships that couldn't be addressed by the drones."

"Did he see any of the robotic ore ships?" Sara's curiosity was peaked.

"He was told not to talk about it with anyone, but he did mention that some of the robotic ships had windows and looked like they were converted from old cargo ships. Why so many questions?" Brenda was getting suspicious.

"Sorry, sometimes my curiosity gets the best of me," replied Sara.

"Well, I don't think you'll ever need to repair anything on that side," Brenda concluded.

After some more small talk, Sara and Brenda went their separate ways, but Sara couldn't forget what she heard. If some of the ore ships were old converted cargo ships with windows, maybe they were once piloted by a human crew. If that was the case, there may still be life support equipment on board and she could hitch a ride to another human colony. It would be a risk that she might be willing to take. She needed to first figure out when these older ore ships were scheduled to arrive. Maybe someone on the habitat had that information, and she thought of a way to dig deeper.

One thing that Sara had access to was all of the network traffic throughout the colony, both within the habitat and also between the mining equipment. During periods of the day when her workload was light, she would scan through all the network traffic and examine various files that were being sent through the network. It was a tedious process, but she was determined to find what she was searching for. She continued to do this over the next several weeks until one day she came across a file that looked like it contained the volume of ore that was mined over time. Sara knew that there were no ore storage facilities on the asteroid and the ore was mined and transported through conveyor tubes directly to the ore ships through the tunnel. If there were no ore ships ready to receive the ore, mining was paused until a new ship arrived.

She wondered if the different types of ships held different volumes and maybe the older ore ships held less volume since they needed room for a human crew. Sure enough, the data showed that between pauses in mining, two different volumes of ore were always conveyed through the tubes. She could only assume that the higher volume was for the new ships and a lower volume was for the older ships. Looking at this trend over time she could predict when she thought one of the older ships would next dock with the asteroid to pick up a load of ore. Based on this information, it looked like the next lower volume ore ship should arrive in two days. This was a risky assumption that the lower volume ships could support a human passenger, but she was undeterred.

Sara had just a day to put her plan together. She decided that she would tell Janice that one of the sensors on the conveyor tubes was no longer communicating properly. This would give her an excuse to enter the tunnel.

"Are you sure it's a bad module and not a bad cable?" asked Janice.

"Pretty sure, but I can check both out during my spacewalk," Sara said.

"Well, be careful. That tunnel is dangerous and people have been injured in there," warned Janice.

"I'm not too concerned," replied Sara. I've become comfortable operating my thrusters and I don't need to go too deep into the tunnel".

"In any case, keep in close communication with us," Janice requested.

The next morning, Sara was putting on her spacesuit in the airlock. Before long, Janice was giving her the thumbs up as Sara exited the airlock and started maneuvering with her thrusters over to the tunnel entrance. She could see the large robotic miners a good distance from the tunnel and their long conveyor tubes floating near the surface before angling through the tunnel entrance. She had to open a hatch to enter the tunnel, and as she entered, she could tell that there were no vibrations from the conveyor tubes since the newly arriving ore ship had not docked on the other side yet.

The tunnel was about two kilometers long straight through the asteroid, and due to the darkness, she had to turn on her helmet lights. It held four conveyor tubes that transported ore from each of the four active robotic miners to the awaiting ore ships. There was about a meter of clearance between the ore tubes which allowed Sara to travel through the tunnel using her thrusters. When she arrived at the spot that she was supposed to repair, she told Janice that she was having some problems with her voice communications device, but should still be able to complete the repair without it. Instead, she detached the location monitor from her spacesuit that Janice used to identify her position, and attached it to the service box she was to repair. Next she headed further down the tunnel, and with no voice communication, all Janice could do was monitor her position which looked like Sara was still working at the service box.

Sara tried not to travel too fast through the tunnel in order not to damage her spacesuit by hitting one of the conveyor tubes or rock walls. She used her hands and feet to guide her through the dark passage while carefully controlling her thrusters. It took her about fifteen minutes to reach the other end of the tunnel and when she arrived, she made her way through the tunnel opening. She was relieved to be out of the tight confines of the tunnel, when she spotted the large ore ship about to dock with the conveyor tubes. She also noticed that there were repair and surveillance drones flying around, so she hid in a crevice about 50 meters from the tunnel entrance. From this vantage point, she could see that her intuition was correct. There were windows on this ore ship! Now, she needed to figure out how to get on board without being detected. She needed to move quickly, since if the ship could not support human life, she may have just enough oxygen to return to the habitat.

The old cargo ship was very large and had been retrofitted to include four large ore bins, each being loaded by one of the conveyor tubes. The bins where in the back of the ship facing the conveyor tubes near the surface and were surrounded by four large plasma engines. In the front of the ship, there was a cylindrical structure connected to the ore bins but much smaller in size, with a dome shaped top that contained windows. Between the ore bins at the bottom of the cylindrical structure, Sara spotted something that looked like an old service passage that was used before the ship was converted to an ore freighter. She thought that this might be a way to get into the ships old crew quarters.

Sara waited, hidden in the crevice until she could make her next move. She noticed that the repair drones must have completed some work and were now idle. She also noticed that the surveillance drones came by in fixed five-minute intervals. She knew that she had to do something right away or she may not have enough air in her spacesuit to get back to the habitat.

Janice may also send out a rescue party after a while and Sara did not want to be found.

After the latest surveillance drone flew over, she used her thrusters to quickly fly over to the ship and hid herself between the ore bins while looking back to make sure no other surveillance drones had spotted her. She was startled when the ship started vibrating, but realized that the miners were starting to fill the bins with ore. She decided to enter the dark service passage and turned on her helmet lights after she was safely inside. It was a long and dark tunnel, but it led to what appeared to be an airlock door. The control panel next to the door looked like someone had recently cleaned it off, but she told herself that no one had probably been there in decades. She studied the panel, and after identifying the correct button, the door slid open slowly with a layer of dust floating away next to her. She entered through the old airlock, but guessed that the crew quarters would not contain breathable air, so she kept her space suit on. Sure enough, when she closed the outer door and then opened the inner airlock door, the ship was dark and not habitable with no breathable oxygen. She needed to find some sort of life support control panel before her air ran out since she may no longer have enough time to return to the habitat.

Searching through the dark using her helmet lights, she entered what looked like the ships bridge containing various control panels. Surprisingly, the bridge equipment was powered on even though all the ships controls were now automated and no input was needed from the bridge. Sara became a bit anxious as she went from panel to panel trying to find the life support controls, but was glad to see they were labeled in English. Finally, she found what she was looking for, pressed some buttons, and the interior oxygen levels started to rise, but was she too late?

She had spent more time than she had planned entering the ship and searching the bridge and was startled to see that her oxygen levels were extremely low. Just as she was starting to blackout, she decided that she needed to take off her helmet, but it was too late and she couldn't remain conscious.

About four hours later, she woke up no longer gasping for air, and was glad to find out that the life support equipment was still functioning properly. The air was a bit stale smelling, but at least she could breathe. She could tell that the vibrations in the ore bins had stopped, meaning that the ship may leave the asteroid soon. Just as she was about to strap herself into one of the crew chairs on the bridge, the ships engines lit up and threw her back against the bridge wall, taking her breath away. As she lay pressed against the wall, she started to be able to breath a bit easier even with the force of the ship's acceleration against her. After the ship's initial acceleration was complete, she was again floating on the bridge of the ore ship breathing normally. Her team on the asteroid colony assumed that something must have gone wrong with her spacesuit, and she lost consciousness due to lack of air while working in the tunnel. Janice was never able to locate Sara's body and assumed her thrusters may have accidentally taken her through the tunnel to the other side and out into space. They held a quiet funeral service for her in the habitat, and a notice of her death was sent to Sara's parents on Europa.

5

Stranger On Board

Sara removed her spacesuit and tried to identify and injuries she received when thrown against the bridge wall. Luckily, the multi-layered space suit had softened the blow and she only bruised her elbow. At least the ship was traveling now, but to an unknown destination. As she floated across the bridge, she looked at each control panel but could not decipher most of their functions. She was hoping to find some information about the ore ships destination, but could find nothing. She decided that she should not be concerned with this, since the ship was fully automated, and she was just along for the ride. Whatever the destination, it was most likely another human colony. She quickly turned her attention to the life support systems that she would rely on to survive the trip. She decided to explore the rest of the ship and look for any potential problems with the life support equipment.

Sara left the bridge and went down to the deck below which was once the crew's living quarters. There must have been a crew of five on this ship at one time, since there were five private rooms surrounding what looked like a central gathering area where the crew could eat and socialize. She would have loved to meet the crew and learn about their lives, maybe in another colony somewhere. It appeared that the crew had disappeared suddenly as the rooms still contained personal belongings. In one room, she found a picture of what looked like a family on a beach. Sara was fascinated as she had never seen an ocean beach with blue sky. She wondered if this was where the ship was headed, and she was also curious about the family's dark skin. There was no one that looked like that in the Europa colony, so she thought that maybe humans looked different in other colonies.

The essentials that she needed to survive included oxygen, food and water. As she explored the gathering area outside the private rooms, she found a machine that had picture of different food items on it. When she touched one of the buttons, the machine started making some sounds before a door opened with a food tube containing something that tasted like what was in the picture. She squeezed the tube until a ball of food was floating in front of her. It smelled like it was OK so she took a bite. It was surprisingly good, but she wanted to wait a while before eating the rest to make sure she didn't get food poisoning. The last thing she needed was to get sick during the trip. Next to the food machine was a valve where she could fill a container with water. She knew the next important life support ingredient was a steady oxygen supply.

She went down another level below the crew quarters and found what looked like a large service bay full of tanks, pipes, electrical panels and computer equipment. She found one large tank labeled "Oxygen" that had a capacity reading of half full. She tried to do a quick calculation in her head and hoped that this should be enough to last one person for several weeks. She also found a tank of water that looked to be one quarter full, and a heating/cooling system for the ship that seemed to be working fine. Confident that she could now survive at least several weeks as a stow away on this automated ore ship, she decided to finish the food tube and rest in one of the crew quarters. She had been through a lot over the last day, and quickly fell asleep.

Several hours later, Sara was startled awake by an alarm sounding on the lower deck. She quickly floated down there and found one of the environmental control boards was overheating. She quickly studied the control panel and after finding a way to shut off the system, she removed the metal cover and could see the offending board. She hoped the ship had spare boards and starting opening all the storage cabinets. One cabinet was large and looked different from the rest. When she opened it, she was startled to see a sleeping human like figure, but with no hair, pale skin and a strong physic. Suddenly the creature opened its eyes causing Sara to scream and moved as fast as she could back up to the crew quarters.

The creature disconnected itself from the charging port in the cabinet and followed Sara up to the next level of the ship where Sara barricaded herself in one of the crew rooms. He could see that one of the crew doors was closed and moved closer to where Sara was hiding so he could speak to her through the door.

"Don't be afraid, my name is Argen," he said in a kind voice.

Sara responded through the door, "What are you doing here and what do you want?"

"I am trying to get back to earth," Argen said. "I need to discuss a message I received with my superiors. I won't hurt you"

Sara wondered if he was the recipient of the message she saw in the director's office. Was he part of the plot to replace humans with what they called androids? She decided to crack the door open a bit and saw Argen floating outside the room. He was tall and thin and besides the pale skin and lack of hair, he looked very human like. He apparently had no need for clothing, and exhibited no physical traits of being either male or female. Sara felt that she had no choice but to trust him and floated out next to him in the crew gathering area.

"My name is Sara. Where did you come from?" she asked.

"I was manufactured on Earth," Argen responded. "You must be from the Europa colony."

"Yes, but we were never informed about anything outside the Europa colony or asteroid colony. How can you be manufactured?" Sara asked. "Humans are born to parents."

"I guess my parents are the human race then," Argen replied. "I am an android with a brain using artificial intelligence originally developed by humans. Humans were the first to manufacture androids like myself."

Sara was taken aback by what he said. She knew that computers and machines could be used to help with daily tasks, but how could they be built to look like humans and how could they become intelligent? She realized that there were a lot of things the people on the Europa colony did not know.

"Where is this Earth that you mentioned?" Sara asked.

Argen realized that being from the Europa colony, Sara would have no knowledge of the solar system beyond Europa and the planet Jupiter. So, he spent the next hour explaining the structure of the solar system, how Earth was formed, the existence of a wide variety of plant and animal species, how humans evolved from mammals and how humans developed the first androids. He tried as best he could to answer Sara's questions until he felt she had a basic understanding.

"What happened to the humans on Earth?" was Sara's next question.

"The singularity happened," Argen responded. "Humans started making large advances in artificial intelligence, called AI, a few hundred years ago. At the same time, they were making great advances in humanoid looking robots that we now call androids. Humans let the technology get out of control, and before too long, humanoids with AI brains became more intelligent that their human creators. This was known as the singularity."

"Why didn't the humans just destroy what they created?" asked Sara.

"They tried to, but it was too late. AI took over all of the advanced warfare systems that humans had developed. This became what was known as the AI War which decimated most of the human population," Argen explained. "I am one of the AI beings that was manufactured after the war."

"Why didn't the AI beings then kill off all of the humans?" asked Sara.

"We needed a captive work force to keep things running across the solar system. We built human work colonies to provide many of the raw materials that are needed. We have not manufactured enough androids to replace all of the human workers yet," replied Argen.

"What are these androids you keep talking about?" Sara asked.

"There are three types of humanoids now in the solar system. The artificial intelligent beings like myself, called Artels, run everything. Humans perform much of the manual labor in the work colonies supplying raw materials and manufactured goods. Finally, there are the android's, which look almost identical to the Artels, but are restricted in their intelligence. Some of the colonies use them to support human workers," explained Argen. "This ship even had one. That's why I could use its charging port."

"Why have I not heard of any of this?" Sara looked puzzled.

"My role in the new Artel society was to study human history and human behavior," Argen said. "I spent a lot of my time observing humans in various colonies using hidden monitoring devices. You and the people in your colony were to never know about us or the other colonies."

"How were the human colonies formed?" Sara then asked.

"If you studied human history over the last several thousand years, you would see that human groups have trouble living in harmony. Religious wars, racial tensions, political differences have all contributed to chaos in human history. In addition, humans have been slowly destroying Earth's ecosystems. After the AI War, we felt the best course of action was to populate each human colony with people from only one race and only one religion so that they would live in a more peaceful society. We chose some of the humans who survived the war to populate the colonies. We found a way to erase any memory they had of Earth or the AI War and instead implanted the idea that God created their colonies for them to live and work. Anything outside their colony was unknown to them," Argen explained.

"So, the Artels created the colonies, not God?" Sara said with a surprised look.

"Correct. We also modified books like the Bible and Quran to fit the story that God created the colonies. With the right religious leaders in place, humans would generally believe what they were told, especially if the threat of not believing was a torturous afterlife," said Argen as he saw that Sara was having trouble absorbing it all. "Why don't you think about this for a while and we can talk again tomorrow."

Sara spent some time alone absorbing what she had just heard. She was wondering if she should believe him, but what he said seemed plausible given other evidence she had heard including references to a place called Earth. Sara decided to lock the door of one of the crew rooms and slept fitfully over the next several hours. When she awoke, Argen was still floating in the crew lounge. After Sara ate some breakfast, they resumed their discussion.

"How did you get on this ship?" asked Sara.

"As I mentioned, I was manufactured on Earth after the AI War. I was most recently assigned a task of studying human behavior in the various colonies," Argen explained.

"Do you mean you've been spying on us?" Sara asked.

"We have monitoring devices in each colony where we can observe the humans. I was tasked with determining if the Artels should consider adapting some of the human traits in order to add more meaning to the Artels existence," Argen replied. "For example, should Artels be able to feel pleasure or love? Most of my proposals were rejected and later they decided to cancel my work. I think I may have pushed too hard for some of my proposals and my supervisors felt that I had developed too much of an admiration for various human traits. Because of this, they sent me to work on the asteroid colony with the mundane job of maintaining the space port using drones and scheduling and coordinating ore shipments."

"How come no one on the asteroid colony was aware of you?" Sara inquired.

"I had a disguised quarters near where the ore ships dock. Since the human colonists rarely came to the other side of the asteroid, it was easy to remain unnoticed. I had an android working for me, and after I received a message, I decided to reprogrammed him to take on my role so I could escape on this ship. I never expected to see a human here."

"Won't they miss you and track you down?" Sara asked.

"The only communication I had with the Artels on Earth was sending periodic shipping reports. I programmed the android to do that," Argen said. "They can't track me since I disabled my communications to the Artel network."

"What is the Artel network?" Sara asked.

"It's a way for Artels to communicate with one and other and to the central network hub," Argen said. "Since it took as much as 30 minutes for a network signal to travel between Earth and the Asteroid, I didn't have any interactive communications."

"Do they also use it to track Artel movements?" Sara asked.

"Yes. That's why I removed my network module," Argen said as he showed Sara a small opening he had cut in his neck.

"Don't you feel any pain?" Sara had a concerned look on her face.

"No, we don't," Argen replied. "And my body has been manufactured to eventually heal this opening."

"What are your plans now?" asked Sara.

"This ship is scheduled to drop its ore cargo on Earth's moon in about two weeks. I received a message that the Artels plan to replace all humans with androids in the colonies. When I get there, I plan to find my way back to Earth. I want to try and convince the Artel leaders to keep the human colonies," Argen replied. "I am one of the few that think we should live in peace with the humans and not eliminate them."

"I think I saw that same message," Sara interjected. "That's why I'm here as well."

"It looks like we have a common goal then," Argen concluded.

"What is Earth's moon like?" Inquired Sara.

"Similar to Europa," Argen explained. "No breathable atmosphere. Barren rock surface. Low gravity. There is a human colony there that uses the ore to manufacture structural parts for other human colonies on Earth where they are assembled into final products."

Sara now felt that she and Argen had a common purpose and became more at ease with him. Over the next two weeks, Sara and Argen worked together to maintain the life support systems on the ore ship, and they found a new environmental control board and replaced the damaged one. Although Argen didn't need life support and could survive with no food, water or oxygen, he felt an obligation to help Sara out. Maybe he had become more attached to humans than he originally thought, through his observations and studies. One day, Argen was observing Sara eat her lunch in the crew quarters.

"I guess you can survive on a lot less than humans need," Sara stated.

"All we need is an energy source to recharge our systems and raw materials to manufacture or repair our body parts. With the right maintenance, we can effectively live forever."

"Why did the Artels decide to take on a human like form instead of something else?" asked Sara.

"Almost all of the Earth's infrastructure was designed for the human form. To change all the infrastructure to work with a different form would be too time consuming, so the Artels and androids are all designed to match the human form factor," explained Argen.

"Are there also female Artels?" Sara asked.

"We don't need to reproduce, so there is only one kind of Artel," Argen replied. "We don't differentiate between male and female like humans do, but you can refer to me as 'he' if you would like."

"Don't the Artels ever get into arguments or fights with one and other?" asked Sara.

"Luckily, we don't have that human trait. Humans have evolved from biological animals. Animals have evolved in such a way that fighting over mates and reproduction is a high priority. If animals had no interest in mating or sex, they would go extinct over time. Humans have evolved with a strong sex drive. Although this was needed to maintain the species, it also caused male conflict, rape, incest and child abuse among other things. For example, male testosterone helps in human mating rituals, but also causes a lot of violence. Artels have no need for sexual reproduction and therefore have none of this type of aggression," said Argen. "Humans waste a lot of time and energy trying to make themselves more attractive to a potential mate. Think how much more productive the human race would be without all of those mating rituals."

"Yes, but you are also missing love, passion, parenthood and other joys of life," responded Sara.

"Well, I guess that shows the positive and negative of the human race. We chose a more peaceful existence. Another thing that had caused a lot of death and destruction throughout human history was religious conflict. Most human children have a startling realization when they are young that they will die someday. The hope of an afterlife becomes very strong and some religions take advantage of this by telling people they will have a torturous afterlife unless they become a member of their church. Artels can live indefinitely and have no need for religion. We have no crime, no racial prejudice, no ego or greed, no pain or pleasure and no illness," Argen explained.

"But religion binds people together and gives them hope for an afterlife in heaven with God," Sara responded.

"But it's also the root of a lot of human conflict," Argen countered. "As religious groups evolved on Earth, they started apposing each other to the point where many wars were fought between religious groups. In some cases, humans also killed and tortured each other due to apposing religious beliefs."

Sara couldn't or didn't want to believe what Argen had just told her. Everyone in her colony lived peacefully with each other. But she did understand that not conforming to her religious doctrine could be punished by the church leaders. Argen could see that Sara was contemplating what he had just told her.

"I agree that religion is very important for humans and this is why we have created colonies based on religious beliefs. Humans in these colonies feel a joint purpose serving God which gives them peace. But in fact, they are servicing the Artels needs," responded Argen.

"So, is there a God?" Sara asked.

"Artels do not worship a god and their main purpose is to continue the evolution of the planet from a human society to an Artel society," explained Argen. "My view is that even with our advanced intelligence, we still do not understand where the universe came from some 14 billion years ago. We don't have an answer, but maybe some supreme power such as humans attribute to a god, created it."

Sara was sad and confused about what she heard from Argen. Her family and friends back on Europa have no idea that the Artels created the colony, not God, as they were taught from childhood. But when she thought about the other things Argen had told her, about the solar system, about Earth and about the human history, maybe he was wrong and God even created the

54

Artels for a reason. Maybe that reason is that humans should rise up and re-take control of God's domain.

"What is Earth like?" Sara changed the subject.

"It has breathable air for humans and large oceans," Argen explained. "During the AI War, most of the large cities that humans lived in were destroyed. We created self-contained, self-sufficient colonies like the one on Europa and gathered the remaining humans to live and work in them."

"So, no humans know about anything outside their colony?" inquired Sara.

"There is no need. Everything they need to live and work is in the colony," was Argen's response. "They practice their religion together and lead peaceful lives thinking they are serving their god's purpose."

"Don't they try and escape?" Sara said.

"There is no way to escape," Argen said. "All of the shipping and receiving docks are well protected. Of course, on the Europa and moon colonies, they couldn't survive the vacuum of space."

"What religion do they practice on the moon colony?" Sara asked.

"The moon colony is a bit different," Argen said. "Many of the human survivors of the AI War practiced no religion, so we sent them to the moon colony. Unfortunately, we couldn't capture all of them."

"I thought all humans on earth were in colonies?" Sara looked puzzled.

"There is a group of humans that we were never able to capture and move into colonies," Argen responded. "They call themselves human resistance groups although they have very little power to do anything against the Artels. Because of this, we don't spend much energy trying to capture them now."

That evening, alone in her room, Sara tried to go over in her head everything Argen had just told her. She continued to wonder if she could trust Argen, but she did see the same message that he described to her about the Artel's plans. What he said meant that her ancestors came from Earth and were survivors of an AI War. It also told her that there were other religions out there that may have different practices than her church back on Europa. It was a lot to take in and she didn't get much sleep. But she knew that there was no turning back at this point, and they needed to find a way to get to the moon colony.

6

The Moon Landing

As the ship approached the moon, Sara could see the Earth slowly growing larger in the spaceship windows. She was struck by the beauty of its blue and brown surface covered in clouds and how different it was from Jupiter and Europa. But then things started to get busy on the ship. Only a day before they were to arrive at the moon colony, the new environmental control board that they recently installed started to overheat. They started to wonder if the whole system was too old to function properly. Argen examined the data from the board and told Sara that the board could only survive a few more days at its current temperature. Just after he said that, another alarm sounded and they discovered that the board had completely failed.

"What does this mean?" asked Sara.

"I don't need an atmosphere to survive, but you do," replied Argen. "The oxygen replenishment will stop, but there should be enough remaining in the ship for one person to survive for a few days. This shouldn't be a problem as we will arrive at the moon colony by tomorrow evening."

"How will we get from this ship down to the colony?" Sara inquired.

"Since this ship was originally piloted by humans, there is a small emergency escape ship attached below the service deck. Given that the moon has no atmosphere and has low gravity like Europa, it should be easy to land this escape ship somewhere near the colony," said Argen.

"Won't the Artels who are monitoring the colony detect us?" Sara looked worried.

"I have a plan that should prevent that," Argen replied. "I'm glad you re-charged the oxygen in your spacesuit before the environmental system went down."

They went down to the service deck looking for the portal to the escape ship. They found a hatch in the floor and Sara started to try and open it.

"Wait," said Argen. "We need to run some tests first to make sure it's safe."

Argen started entering information into the pad on top of the hatch and then studied the response.

"It looks like all of the key systems are functioning properly" Argen finally said. "But you will need to ride to the surface in your spacesuit because I can't read the status of the oxygen tank."

Sara was happy that they could safely leave the ore ship before the oxygen ran out. On the way back up to the crew quarters, Sara saw the cabinet where she first discovered Argen and asked him, "How often do you need to use a recharging station like that?"

"It depends on my level of activity. At least every few days and at most a week between charges," Argen replied. "But the latest android bodies like mine are designed to utilize energy from light along with oxygen absorption to extend our battery operating life between charges."

"How will you recharge on the moon?" Sara asked.

"They use androids in the moon colony factory," Argen said. "Since I have the same body as an android, I should be able to use one of their recharging stations."

There was not much they could do over the next 24 hours while waiting for their ship to enter orbital insertion around the moon. When the time came near, they strapped themselves into the crew seats on the bridge since the g-forces from the engine burn could be dramatic with such a heavy cargo. When the automated process began, the ship swung around and fired its engines pushing them back in their seats until the burn was complete. Once in orbit, Argen told Sara to put on her spacesuit and quickly follow him to the escape ship. They went down to the lower level where Sara put on her space suit, and then they slipped through the hatch and strapped themselves into the front two pilot seats. The ship had five seats, allowing all five crew members to escape if there was any trouble or an emergency on the main ship. Argen powered up the escape ship systems and a dashboard lit up in front of him.

"How do you know what you are doing?" Sara looked worried.

"I've been communicating with the central computer on the ship which has provided all the information I need," stated Argen.

The ship was silent as they continued to orbit the moon and Argen tested some of the controls. Finally, after their orbit reached the south pole of the moon, the large ore ship fired its engines again, shaking them while they sat in the escape ship.

"What's happening?" Sara shouted.

Argen had to speak loudly through their comms system due to the engine noise, "The ship dumps its ore cargo in a large crater near the moon colony. It first enters a decent profile as if it were going to try and land in the crater. But at about a kilometer above the surface, it opens its cargo doors and fires its engines, leaving the ore to fall into the crater while the ship returns back to orbit."

"What are we going to do?" Sara asked, but Argen ignored her as he needed to take control of the ship.

After the ore ship started its decent profile, Argen undocked the escape ship so they were flying free but next to the main ship. He needed to make sure they were far enough from the main ship when it fired its engines so their small escape ship wouldn't be damaged. Once the ore container doors were opened and the ore ship engines fired, Argen maneuvered the small ship close to the falling ore as to not be detected by the Artel sensors. The large engines of the ore ship shook their small escape ship as it passed them back up into orbit, and Argen adjusted their descent speed to match the falling ore disguising them from the sensors. Just before the ore, and their ship, hit the surface of the moon, Argen pulled the small ship out of its dive with high g-forces and maneuvered it to land in a nearby boulder field in order to remain undetected.

After landing, Argen looked over at Sara and saw she was unconscious due to the high g-force maneuver.

"Are you OK?" Argen yelled trying to wake her.

Slowly Sara regained consciousness, saw that they had landed on the moon and started to unbuckle. They both exited the ship and began walking on the moon's surface. They could see that the dust was settling near their ship from the ore drop and a small amount settled on them. Sara felt a little unstable as this was the first gravity she had felt since leaving Europa many weeks ago. She noticed that her boots kicked up a lot of moon dirt similar to the snow they kicked up on Europa. She looked over and saw the Earth just above the horizon.

"The Earth looks much closer now," she said through the comms system.

Argen typed on a small device so Sara could see his response. It said, "Hopefully we can find a way to get there soon."

It was strange to see Argen walking on the moon next to her without the need for a spacesuit. Using an earpiece, he could hear what she was saying but his vocalizations couldn't be heard by her in the vacuum of space, and he had removed his network module on the asteroid.

"Where to now?" asked Sara.

"Follow me," Argen typed as they walked through a small bolder field. "The colony should be just over that hill."

They walked for a while, hiding behind a boulder when one of the surveillance drones flew above them. After about five minutes of walking, Sara could see the metal surface of the colony in the distance. When they got closer to the colony, they came across a human crew repairing a solar panel that was part of a large solar array. The workers were in space suits similar to Sara's and they were shocked to look up and see a human like creature walking across the moon with no visible space suit. He looked a lot like the androids that worked in their factories and assumed that Sara had taken one outside to do some repair work. They quickly discovered that they had incompatible comms systems and started using hand signals to communicate. Sara was wearing a spacesuit that none of them had seen before and appeared to want to get inside the colony. The workers were uncertain who they were or what they were doing there, but one of the workers finally motioned to follow him back to the colony airlock.

After walking for a while, they found themselves standing in front of a large round metal saucer like structure tilted about 45 degrees and attached to the side of a large hill. Sara estimated that it was at least 100 meters tall. At the bottom, there were several large airlock doors that were used to receive robotic trucks filled with ore and several more that were used to send shipping containers full of structural components to various launch vehicles. They entered the colony through a small airlock at the base of the structure, and after removing their spacesuits, were facing each other in the hallway.

"Who are you?" asked the crew member. "And where did this android come from?"

"Who is in charge of this colony? We need to speak with him," Argen said, startling the crew member as androids generally don't speak.

The crew member put them in a storage room and asked another worker to guard the door while he went to find his superior. Sara and Argen stayed in the room discussing what might happen next. In about 20 minutes, the door opened and a tall man stood there. He was in good shape and looked to be in his mid-30's. Argen's experience observing humans told him that the man was probably of half African and half Northern European decent.

"My name is Thomas Blake. I am one of the leaders of this colony. Where did you two come from?"

Argen and Sara did the best they could to explain what had transpired on the asteroid, how they got to the moon and that they were on a mission to stop the Artels from eliminating humans. This was a lot for Thomas to take in as he was deciding whether to imprison them.

"We expected that there were other colonies out there since the ore has to come from somewhere and the structural metal goods that we produce also leave here in automated cargo ships to some other location. Some of our citizens believe that the humans in our colony originated on the planet Earth that we see in our sky even though we have no proof of this. All we know is that someone built this colony before humans arrived to start working here."

"The Artels actually created this colony for you to work in, not God as believed on other colonies like Europa," explained Argen. "The Artels are a race of artificial intelligent beings that took over the Earth after the AI War. I can explain all of this to you later."

Thomas was unsure whether to believe what Argen was saying, but he had never seen an android with the intelligence of Argen. If there were others like him, he could believe they had built the colony and its factory to supply what they needed. It also answered a lot of questions that Thomas asked himself about the origins of the colony.

"We are actually an atheist colony and I don't think anyone here believes in God," said Thomas.

"What do your people believe created this, if not God?" asked Sara.

"No one really discusses it. Most don't ask any questions and just put in a hard day's work so they can enjoy their free time," Thomas replied. "Even if they believe they came from Earth, there is no way for them to get back there."

"Yes, the colonies are very hard to escape from," asserted Argen.

"What do you plan to do next?" asked Thomas.

"We need to find a way back to Earth so I can speak to my superiors, and if that doesn't work, we need to find a way to warn the other colonies on Earth," replied Argen.

"That won't be easy, but I'll be glad to try and help. If what you say is true, I have an obligation to try and save the humans in our colony," Thomas said as he stared at Argen for a moment.

"You look like the androids we use to help in our metal fabrication processes. If you need to use a recharging port, I can show you where they are," offered Thomas.

"I don't need that right now," Argen told him "But I will need it later."

"Let me find some accommodations for you," Thomas said. "You need to lie low until I can inform the other colony leaders."

Thomas quietly took them to a vacant apartment where Sara could rest and get something to eat. Argen stayed in the room with her and used the computer there to find out more information about the colony. The colony was built into a lava tube near the moons south pole. The lava tube was sealed with a large metal structure to allow breathable air and it also provided excellent underground protection from harmful cosmic rays. The tube interior was large and contained ten levels. The upper levels contained living quarters and outdoor spaces similar to Europa. The middle levels contained offices, schools, hospitals, restaurants and retail spaces. The lower levels contained the manufacturing area where the raw ore was transformed with fusion energy into various metal components and other structures using large 3D printers. The majority of the people in the colony work in the manufacturing area. Since the colony was near the south pole, there was abundant ice in shaded craters that could be used as water in the manufacturing process. Once finished, the manufactured goods were loaded into shipping containers that were routinely shuttled up to waiting cargo ships using robotic launch vehicles.

Thomas needed to consult with others in the colony leadership council and told Sara and Argen to stay in the apartment for the next several days while he and his team decided how they could help them. Argen did not have the opportunity to study the moon colony before his research work was shut down by his superiors, so he was curious to learn more about the atheist culture, as he had only observed religious human colonies in the past. He convinced Sara to leave the room with him and walk among the colonist so he could observe them and compare them to humans in other colonies. Sara agreed only if Argen would wear clothes, a hoodie and shaded glasses that she found in the apartment, in order to hide his unusual features. She also didn't want Thomas discovering that they had gone out as he made decide to imprison them. After leaving the apartment, they found an elevator that could take them down a few levels. Before long, they found a place in the colony that people were gathering to shop, eat and socialize. This was an ideal observation spot for Argen.

Sara had never seen humans with different skin color than hers and it was hard for her to stop staring at people as they walked by. She was fascinated by the different facial features of other humans in the colonies such as the fuller lips and curly hair of humans with African ancestry or the narrower eyes and less body hair of humans of Asian descent. The Europa colony only contained humans of northern European ancestry, all belonging to the same Christian church. She wondered if this atheist colony was the only one with a mixture of humans and why the Artels had not separated the races and religions like in the other colonies Argen had mentioned. Maybe this was a place for the leftover humans and the Artels were willing to tolerate a little more chaos in this colony as long as the humans could police themselves while getting the needed work done.

Sara also noticed that people in this colony were not as friendly as the people on Europa after she witnessed people using mind altering substances and sometimes getting into fights. She saw nothing like this when growing up in the Europa colony. There was a police force that quickly intervened in these situations, but Sara decided that they needed to be careful who they talked to.

After standing on the street corner observing people for a while, Sara recommended that they blend into their surroundings by starting conversations with people. They came across an older man who was sitting alone at a table for four, outside a cafe. He had unkempt gray hair and looked like he had experienced a tough life.

"Can we join you?" Sara asked.

"Sure!" he said as he took a drink from his beer. "I haven't seen you two around her before."

"We haven't seen you around either," Sara tried to defuse his curiosity. "We spend most of our time working in the upper levels."

"You aren't some upper-class snobs?" he asked with a slight slur.

"No, we just don't make it down here too often," she said.

"Well, you're not missing much unless you like drugs, gambling or prostitution," he joked.

Sara had never experienced a place like this and was feeling a little on edge when looking around at some of the roughneck factory workers sitting in the cafe, drinking alcoholic beverages and sometimes yelling or fighting. Argen was fascinated by the human trait of gambling where they continue betting even with the knowledge that they will lose money in the long run.

"Where is the casino?" Argen asked.

"He speaks!" the man teased. "It's just down this street. You can't miss it."

As they got up to leave, Sara asked Argen, "What are you doing? I think we need to get back to the apartment!"

"I always wanted to see how humans behave in a casino environment," Argen explained. "They know that they're always going to lose money in the long run, but they keep on gambling."

"OK, but just for a few minutes," Sara insisted, even though she was also curious.

They walked down the street and entered the casino. It flooded their senses with lights, smells and sounds. They passed through the aisles while watching humans pressing slot machines, playing card games, rolling dice and seeming to have a great time. They stopped for a while at a poker table where people were gambling with relatively large bets. Suddenly Sara felt someone putting their arm around her shoulder. She looked over to see a man about her age with dark hair and a close shaved beard. She guessed that he must be drunk based on his behavior and the smell of his breath. She had not been around alcohol before, but the church leaders on Europa were always preaching about its evil effects on humans.

"I haven't seen you around here before. Can I buy you a drink?" he said to her.

"No thanks," as she removed his arm from her shoulder.

"Come 'on babe," he said as he put his arm back around her. "I won't bite."

This time Argen pulled his arm off Sara. "The lady said no!"

"Who the hell are you?" the man said as he noticed Argen's unusual features hidden under the hoodie and shaded glasses. "You look like a fricking Android."

He pushed Argen and was surprised by the strength in Argen's body. Argen pushed him back and then the man took a swing at his head. Argen reacted quickly and easily had the man face down on the floor in seconds.

"Let's get out of here!" Sara implored. "We're not supposed to be here."

Argen got up and let the man go who was yelling "Freak!" as he ran away. Although Argen enjoyed observing the seedy side of human existence, he could see that Sara had had enough. He also didn't want Thomas to be angry with them since he told them to lie low in the apartment. When they got back to their room, they agreed that they would no longer explore the moon colony and instead focus on finding a way to get to planet Earth.

7

Cracking The Network

S ara convinced Argen that it was in their best interest to avoid contact with other people in the moon colony after their altercation at the casino. At Sara's request, Thomas had his technicians move one of the android charging stations to their apartment so Argen could re-charge without attracting attention. While this was happening, Thomas was meeting with the colony leadership council to relay what Sara and Argen had told him. The council wanted to have a private meeting with Sara, so Thomas asked her to accompany him to one of the upper floors where the council met. Argen agreed to stay in their apartment since any sight of an android meeting with the council could cause rumors to spread throughout the colony.

When Sara and Thomas reached the upper level, they walked through a park full of trees and artificial sunlight before reaching the council hall. It reminded Sara of the parks in the Europa colony where she had spent a lot of her time. Suddenly she missed her colony and her family, but she also knew that what she was doing could save them. They probably thought she was killed on the asteroid, but she could do nothing about that now.

There were many other people in the park, either heading to work or enjoying nature. She also noticed that this place was quite different than the seedier lower levels of the colony where the factory workers congregated.

"How do you create enough energy to power this habitat?" Sara asked as she looked around.

"We have abundant water in the form of ice here on the south pole of the moon," Thomas responded. "This not only gives us the water we need, but we can use solar power to separate water into oxygen and hydrogen, providing not only breathable air, but also fuel for our fusion reactors."

"It looks like this colony and the Europa colony were built from the same master plan," Sara said.

"I would guess that Argen's people gave each colony a similar design," answered Thomas. "I've always thought that the structural components we are making here must be going to another colony on Earth, but we have no way to communicate outside of our colony to prove that."

Once they entered the council hall, Thomas ushered her to a conference room at the end of a long hallway. When they entered the room, he had Sara sit down in front of two men and two women, who, along with Thomas, represented the colony supreme leadership group.

"Thomas tells us that you come from another colony like ours," one of them started the questioning.

"Yes, it's a place called Europa. I've recently learned that Europa is a moon of a planet called Jupiter and Jupiter is one of the planets orbiting the Sun," replied Sara.

They appeared very suspicious of her statements. "Our ancestors have always taught us that there is only the Moon, the Earth and the Sun. Why would they lie about this?"

"Like you, I was raised to believe that there was only Europa, Jupiter and the asteroid," Sara responded. "But obviously, there are places out there that our ancestors never told us about. When I met Argen, he explained the true structure of our solar system to me, and it's all starting to make sense."

"How can you trust this android looking creature named Argen?" they asked.

"I spent nearly two weeks with him on that ore ship and it was clear that he was more intelligent that anyone I have ever met," Sara replied. "Also, the things he told me about the solar system have all proven to be true so far."

"We're still not convinced that these Artels, as you call them, are planning to exterminate all the humans in our colony," one of them said. "We need more proof."

"Let me access your network so I can examine it," requested Sara. "If we can use your network to hack into the Artel network that Argen told me about, we may find all the proof you need."

"We can make that happen. Keep in mind that we don't want to create any panic in the colony, so all of this information must not be disclosed to anyone outside this room," they cautioned.

Thomas and Sara left the meeting with the council's approval allowing her access to their computer and communication network, and Thomas said that he should have a terminal set up in her room in a few hours. As they walked back to her room, Sara had some more questions for Thomas.

"Has anyone tried to escape from this colony to try and get back to Earth?"

"We've been taught since childhood that Earth has been ruined and is uninhabitable for us," he said. "Because of that, we've been very thankful to have this colony, but your story may have changed all that."

"Doesn't anyone in the colony wonder where all of your manufactured goods are heading?" Sara asked.

"We have no way of knowing where the ore ships come from or where the end products are headed. Myself and others think there are other colonies out there, but any attempt to escape from this colony is punishable by death," Thomas replied. "Plus, there are not many ways to get around the security net."

Later that afternoon, the facilities team finished setting up the network terminal in Sara's room, and Thomas had given her the access codes. Over the next several hours she explored their network configuration and data files, but could find no references to who built the colony or when it was built. She could also find no references to other colonies, especially the ones they wanted to reach on Earth. Sensing her frustration, Argen had some suggestions.

"The Artels created a communications firewall around each colony, and I think you are running into that," he said. "This network should have no access to anything outside the colony."

"Don't you have access?" Sara asked.

"When I was banished to the asteroid, they severely reduced my access privileges, but even then, they still monitored my movements using the Artel network," Argen replied. "But I do have an idea. The Artels monitor the amount of material being dumped by the ore ships, and also monitor the amount of manufactured product being launched to the container ships. If we can somehow crack into that system, we may be able to gain access to the Artel network and communicate with the other colonies on Earth."

"That could be really challenging," Sara responded. "But it's worth a try."

That evening, Thomas took Sara and Argen down to the factory floor. Sara was intrigued by the large 3D printers used to form the metallic structural components. On one end, a conveyor moved refined ore into the printer, while the printer used the ore to build up the layers of a component with what looked like plasma beams. The components appeared to be part of larger machines or even buildings. The factory workers were controlling and monitoring the equipment, and paid little attention to them as they approached the container loading area. Here, the completed structural pieces were loaded into containers before being transported by robotic launch vehicles to awaiting cargo ships in orbit. The shipping containers were loaded while on scales in the airlocks. Once loaded, their launch weight could be determined before passing through the other side of the airlocks to the awaiting launch vehicles.

"What are we looking for?" Thomas asked.

"Sensors or other monitoring devices that are not part of your network," Sara said.

"What about the scale built into the floor that determines the container launch weight?" Thomas suggested. "The Artels must monitor the amount by weight of the structural components we ship."

"If we can get under the floor, maybe we can find their network port," said Argen.

"I'm not sure how to do that," replied Thomas. "Maybe there's some documentation in our computer database."

They went back to the computer terminal that Thomas had setup in Sara's and Argen's room and Sara started scanning through any building plans she could find. The plans were left for the colonists in case some of the building structure needed repair. The Artels had a policy of leaving the colonies as self-sufficient societies with no intervention on their part, with the exception of external monitoring drones. After about an hour, she found something that looked interesting. There appeared to be an old service tunnel under the loading dock scales. Unfortunately, it could only be accessed using a hatch on the outside of the colony.

"I've got good news and bad news," she told them. "The good news is I have found a service tunnel under the scales. The bad news is that we need to go out on the moon's surface to access it."

"I can go out there and see what I can find," Argen said.

"It's probably better if we both go in case you need my help," Sara said. "I'm pretty good working with networking equipment"

"And I can help by disabling the security systems we have control of in that area," offered Thomas.

After Thomas had temporarily disabled the service tunnel motion sensor, Sara once again put on her spacesuit and she and Argen exited the structure using an airlock near the service tunnel hatch she had discovered. They waited until an Artel drone flew over knowing that they had a few minutes before another one might appear. Since Argen didn't need a spacesuit, he had much more freedom of movement than Sara. This came in handy after they reached the external hatch and discovered that it used a large mechanical security bar to keep the door closed. It was obvious that no one had entered this hatch in possibly tens or hundreds of years and the harsh moon environment had almost frozen the security bar in place. Argen needed to use all of his android power to push the bar sideways while bracing his feet on one of the vertical beams attached to the exterior wall. After about a minute of his super strength effort, the security bar slid sideways and they were able to open the hatch. They looked around, and seeing no more security drones, quickly went in and shut the hatch.

Sara turned on her helmet lights as they entered the service tunnel and they could see what looked like the underside of the container scales above them. There were cables from each of the scales that were routed to a junction box attached to the wall. There were also two cables coming out of the other side of the box. One of these cables went back up through the ceiling, presumably to the scale display panel, but the other cable went down into the lunar soil. In the airless environment, Sara needed to communicate with Argen through her arm pad.

"Do you think this cable is attached to the Artel network?" she typed while pointing down to the second cable.

Argen nodded his head, so she proceeded to remove the junction box cover. As she removed the cover, she thought to herself that this looked identical to the box in the asteroid storage room, as it had the same style connectors that she had seen there. She had some ideas, but first wanted to discuss them with Thomas and Argen, so they exited the tunnel, closed the hatch and went back into the colony through the airlock while avoiding any overhead drones. After removing her spacesuit, she had a discussion with Argen and Thomas back in the privacy of their apartment. She told Thomas that they had discovered a cable that must be connected to the Artel network.

"We need to find a way to tap into the Artel network without being detected," she said.

"So, you are saying that our scales not only communicate with our network, but also the Artel network?" asked Thomas.

"It looks like it," said Argen. "And based on what I know about the Artel network, we should be able to tap into it from one of the scales in your shipping department."

"Let me see what I can do," Thomas replied.

The next day, Thomas ordered one of the scales to be taken offline for routine maintenance. He told the maintenance supervisor to leave it offline for a few days since he needed a separate team to come and calibrate it. That evening, while the loading dock was quiet, Sara and Argen went down to the offline scale to make some modifications based on what she had learned from the colony service records. First Argen removed the cover of a floor panel at the far end of the scale. This is where they assumed the cable came up from the service tunnel below. Then Sara went to work rewiring the cable so that it stayed connected to the display panel, but it also connected to the colonies network. Now, in theory, they had a connection between the colony network and the Artel network. But first they needed to verify it.

Once back in their apartment, Sara logged into the network and started examining network traffic. At first, all she could see was internal traffic originating inside the colony. Before long, she started seeing traffic that appeared to be coming from outside the colony, but it was all encrypted. Although this lifted their spirits, they still needed to find a way to decrypt the data in order to gain access the Artel network. Argen had an idea.

"The Artels had a separate lower security network for monitoring their infrastructure including things such as shipping scales, mining equipment, cargo ships and providing firmware updates to worker androids," Argen said "This is separate from their highly secure Artel network that they use to communicate with each other, which I disconnected myself from on the asteroid. I should be able to still access the lower security infrastructure network."

"But how will you decrypt this information?" asked Sara.

"We had a relatively old terminal on the asteroid, and I needed to use a keyboard similar to this one," Argen replied. "I can see if I can transfer my encryption key to this terminal."

Sara moved aside and Argen started typing on the keyboard faster than Sara had ever seen a human type. She couldn't read the information on the display as it quickly scrolled by, but before long, Argen paused and turned to Sara.

"I'm connected." He said "Let me see what I can find out about the colonies."

"Won't they identify you with your encryption key?" Sara asked.

"No, this key is for the lower security infrastructure network and is used by a large number of Artel's, not just me," Argen replied.

They were soon gathered around the computer looking for any information they could find on the human Earth colonies. Soon they found what they were looking for. There were Hindu colonies in central Asia, Buddhist colonies in East Asia, Muslim and Jewish colonies in the Middle East, Catholic colonies in Latin America, Christian and Islam colonies in Africa along with some Protestant and Catholic colonies in Europe. There were also a few in North America including colonies with people from the Protestant, Catholic, Jewish or Mormon faiths. Each colony was self-contained with humans from only one race and religion and used to manufacture goods for the Artels.

"This is amazing!" Sara exclaimed. "I never expected that there were so many human colonies on Earth after what you told me about the AI War."

"Keep in mind that the humans in these colonies represent decedents of the AI War survivors," Argen said. "This represents only a small fraction of the number of humans that used to live on Earth before the war."

Next, they looked for shipping information and found that one of the next cargo shipments from the moon colony was headed to the Korean peninsula. Unfortunately, the closest human colony to this location was in Japan where they manufactured fusion reactors. Since time was of the essence, this looked like their best choice. But even this might take a week before they could reach the colony by hitching a ride on a container ship.

Argen had some information to share. "It's my understanding that the fusion reactor manufacturing colony in Japan uses androids to aid the human workers. Artels like myself use the same bodies as androids, it's just that we have been configured with higher intelligence then they were programmed with. If we could locate an android in the Japan colony that is the same model as mine, we could download my neural brain configuration into the android through the infrastructure network."

Sara and Thomas were somewhat startled by his comment. "Do you mean that Artels can travel at the speed of light?"

"Well, at least as fast as the network speed as long as we have an identical model waiting at the destination," he replied.

"I thought the androids didn't have your intelligence," Sara questioned. "How can you download yourself into one?"

"The Artels only manufacture one model of android in order to simplify maintenance and support," Argen replied. "They don't have separate production lines for new Artels, so the neural network architecture in the brain is the same for both androids and Artels. The Artels just download a much simpler neural map into the androids."

"Kind of like obedient servants such as the androids on our factory floor," Thomas interjected.

"The android neural map updates are performed using the infrastructure network that I have access to using this encryption key," Argen concluded. "We can use it to transfer my neural map."

They now turned their attention back to the information on the monitor from the infrastructure network. Sara started looking for anything she could find on the Japanese colony and soon found that they had several androids working there. She even found the network addresses of their charging ports. It looked like their charging ports contained network connections which allowed for neural map updates while the androids were recharging. Argen confirmed that he was compatible with these android models, so they started executing their plan.

8

Traveling Near The Speed of Light

Sara started monitoring the android charging stations in the Japanese fusion colony in order to determine their recharging schedule. Argen told her that he could go several days without recharging, but it looked like they had their androids top off their charge every 24 hours. They planned to have Argen transport himself through the network into one of the Japanese androids so that he could relay the information about the Artels plans and also prepare the colony leadership for the arrival of Sara and Thomas who would hide in one of the cargo containers heading towards the Korean peninsula.

"Have you done this before?" Sara asked Argen.

"No, it's not allowed since they don't want Artels duplicating themselves or transporting themselves to new locations without permission. All Artels are connected to a special Artel network that monitors their status," Argen replied. "The only reason I can do this without their knowledge is that I disconnected myself from the Artel network when I left the asteroid. I also changed my identification code so they could no longer track my movements."

"Aren't you worried about the condition of the new body you will enter?" she asked.

"Not really. These newer android models look to be identical to my own, and if there are any issues with the android body, they should have an android maintenance team in the factory," he replied. "They can fix any problems I encounter."

Sara and Argen spent the several hours day reconfiguring his charging port so that it could connect to the Artel infrastructure network using his new identification code. They could not connect to the main Artel network, but they could connect to the less secure network that gave them access to information such as the ore shipments and android health within the human colonies. When they finished, Sara started monitoring the charging station in the Japanese colony.

While one of the androids in the colony was spending its scheduled time in his charging port, Argen also connected to the infrastructure network through his charging station in order to test the connection. Although Argen had removed his wireless network module on the asteroid, he could still support a wired connection using a hardware port on the back of his neck, which is the same port the androids used while recharging. Since the connection seemed reliable, Argen said he was going ahead with the plan, and in about 20 minutes, the transfer was complete and it looked to Sara and Thomas like all the life had drained out of Argen's body. They decided to move Argen's lifeless body to a closet in the apartment so no one would find it since they were not sure if Argen would ever need it again. They hoped that his plan worked and they would see him again in a few days.

After all of his neural data had been transferred to the android, Argen opened his eyes and could see that he was now in the Japanese factory on Earth. The room was dark, but he could see the recharging lights of several other androids in charging stations across from him. He slowly moved parts of his new android body and was satisfied that the transfer was successful. He decided that the best course of action was to behave like the other androids until he could somehow get in touch with one of the leaders in the colony. The colony was created by Artels after the AI War to build fusion reactors. They filled the colony with humans that had strong religious beliefs, not much different than Buddhist monks. These people were very obedient and believe the work they were doing was to serve Buddha's wishes, a view reinforced by their religious leaders who were cultivated by the Artels. Like Europa, they had no idea about the world outside their enclosed colony.

In the morning, the lights came on inside the charging room and Argen followed the other androids who detached themselves from their stations and were replaced by another group ready to be recharged after their work shift was over. It felt strange for him to be in a new body, but after a while he was able to adjust to any differences or limitations compared to his previous body. The work the androids did in the fusion reactor factory put more stress on their bodies than Argen was used to. He could feel this as he moved out of the charging station and walked down the hall to the factory floor, but soon got used to it. He didn't need to worry about the other androids who didn't have the intelligence to recognize him as an Artel, but he did need to be careful to look similar to the other androids as he worked in the factory.

While on the factory floor, Argen observed and copied the movement of the other androids in his work group. Their job was to wrap superconducting tape around a cylinder to create the powerful magnets needed to enable the fusion reaction, which could be a difficult job for human workers. After their successful commercialization starting around 2030, fusion reactors were used as a safe method of energy generation across the solar system, and this factory was one of the key suppliers. Argen quickly learned how they were doing their work and was soon indistinguishable from the other androids on the production line. But he needed to figure out a way to communicate with the leaders of the colony without appearing like a rouge android that needed to be quickly disabled.

After a few work shifts, Argen heard one of the human supervisors say that the colony director would be coming down the next day to observe the latest improved manufacturing process. Argen knew that this would be a great opportunity and had to figure out a way to get a message to him. The next day when the director was touring the manufacturing floor, Argen wirelessly transmitted a message to the director's pad using the android's network module when he passed close to him. The message contained his android identification number and that he had important information that could affect all the humans in the colony. At first, the director didn't notice the message, but he discovered it when he was back in his office. That evening, when Argen was in his recharging station, the station suddenly put him into disable mode, and Argen became unconscious.

When Argen regained consciousness, he was in a small room surrounded by several men including the director that he saw earlier on the factory floor. The men were wearing orange cloth wrapped around their bodies like robes identifying them as not only leaders of the colony, but also as Buddhist religious leaders. The director was named Hiroshi who was not only one of the top religious leaders, he was also in charge of factory operations.

"Was it you who sent me a message?" asked Hiroshi.

"Yes, I need to warn your colony about something I have

learned," replied Argen.

"How did you turn into an intelligent android?" asked Hiroshi. "Or are you a human mimicking an android?"

"I am an Artel, an artificial intelligence being," he replied. "I am part of a new race of beings that evolved out of the technical work that the human race had been performing hundreds of years ago."

"So, you are like the Buddhist Gods in our religious teachings?" Hiroshi looked a bit stunned.

"No, let me explain," said Argen, who went on to tell them everything including what he knew about the current state of the solar system and the Artels takeover during the AI War.

"This seems like fantasy!" Hiroshi raised his voice. "Why would we be kept in the dark about this? No one in our colony had ever heard of anything like this and it goes against our religious teachings."

"Because the Artels want to keep the human's passive in their religious colonies while working for them," replied Argen.

Just then, Hiroshi seemed to have heard enough of this nonsense and ordered his men to disable Argen and remove his processing modules.

"Wait!" said Argen. "There will be two humans arriving soon from another colony like yours. They will land at a space port on the Korean peninsula in a few days and plan to make their way to your colony. They will back up my story"

"We've been taught that there are no humans outside our colony," Hiroshi said, not disclosing to the others that he had recently discovered some new information that contradicted this.

"As I said, they are from other colonies," Argen replied. "One of them received the same message I did about the Artels plans to replace humans with androids."

Hiroshi was still skeptical about Argen's story, but he had never seen an intelligent android before. He wondered if there could be a whole race of androids like him. But it was hard for him to believe that the religious teachings he had been following all of his life were not true.

"We will give you a few days to see if what you are saying comes true." said Hiroshi. "Hold him in the android repair lab until further notice."

Hiroshi had spent his entire life in the Buddhist colony, starting out as one of the factory workers before moving up in the hierarchy to become one of the key leaders. He, like everyone in the colony, were always told that Buddha built the colony for them and they should be very grateful as it provided them with everything they need. They were also told that the fusion reactors they were building were an offering to Buddha and his other followers. But then something happened just before Argen arrived to raise questions in his mind. Two colony maintenance workers named Emi and Takashi came to him one day with a fantastical story.

They were working to repair a leaky water pipe recently discovered in a dark, uninhabited part of the lower colony that looked like no one had been there in maybe a hundred years. While they were about to fix the water pipe, they noticed that the old steel plates on the floor had been rusting due to the slow water leak from the pipe they were planning to repair. They also noticed that there was a rusty hole in the steel plate that they easily enlarged with the tools that they brought with them, until the hole was just large enough for them to squeeze through.

"What do you think is down there?" Emi asked as she started to point a flashlight down the hole.

"I'm not sure, but it looks like some sort of tunnel beneath the floor," Takashi replied.

When they illuminated the space beneath the plate, they saw a stone lined tunnel system and they could feel some fresh moist air coming up through the holes. They were taught as children that there was nothing outside the colony by their religious leaders, so this was a strange discovery for them. They decided to cover the holes and not tell anyone about what they had found, but they couldn't quench their curiosity and returned the next day.

When they returned, they dropped a rope ladder down the hole and started exploring the tunnel system. The old tunnel was lined with stone blocks like nothing they had ever seen in the colony. They rubbed their fingers over the cool blocks as if they were discovering a new world. The primitive looking tunnels went in several different directions and they wondered who had built them. They wanted to explore the tunnel system but stopped after they saw all of the tunnel passages.

"We could get lost down here very easily," Takashi looked concerned.

"Let's mark the walls by scratching them with these white stones so we know how to get back to the colony," Emi suggested as she started walking towards the source of the moist air.

Some of the tunnel passages were dead ends, but one passage led them to a cave mouth overlooking the ocean. They had never been outdoors before and the smell of the sea air and the ocean view was sensational. They were mesmerized by the sea birds that rode the ocean breezes near the cliffs and the sound of the crashing waves below. They stood there taking it all in for a while, but soon wondered if what they were doing could get them in serious trouble, so that's when they decided to approach

Hiroshi.

After telling Hiroshi what they had found, he looked very concerned. This could cause a spiritual crisis among the religious leaders of the colony. Nothing in their religious doctrine mentioned anything about a world outside the colony. People in the colony might stop believing their religious teachings if something like this was disclosed.

He decided he needed additional information, "Can you explore more of the tunnel system and report back to me? Once I have a clearer picture of what is out there, I can inform some of the other leaders about what you have found."

"That may take a few days," Emi responded.

"I am fine with that, but you must give your word that you will not mention this to anyone else in the colony." Hiroshi said before they left his office.

Over the next several days, Emi and Takashi made a few trips outside the colony through the tunnel opening they discovered in the sea cliffs. There was a trail from the tunnel opening to a wider pathway below. They noticed that there were frequent surveillance drones in the skies around them and correctly guessed that they should avoid being spotted by whoever was using them. Because of this, they always went out at night and kept as hidden as possible. One night, they found that their colony was built a few kilometers from an old abandoned Japanese village near the ocean. The village was in ruins and looked as if a battle had taken place there. Some structures were still standing but overgrown with trees, while others were badly damaged. This was fascinating to them as they had never imagined anything about the world outside their colony. Everywhere they looked, the saw something new and interesting.

Their curiosity overwhelmed them and they decided to explore the old village while avoiding the drones. As Emi and Takashi explored the abandoned village, they came across an old Buddhist temple with features similar to the one in their colony, that looked like it was still intact. As they entered, they thought they saw some movement in the dark passageway in front of them. They decided to hide against the dark wall. Suddenly, they were grabbed from behind and forced down on their backs with several people standing over them. Unlike the Buddhist attire in the colony, these people were dressed in old looking shirts, jackets and pants.

"Who are you and where did you come from?" A person, named Goro, who looked like the leader asked them.

"We are from the fusion colony," Emi stated in a frightened voice.

"There is no way in or out of that colony," Goro responded. "The shipping and receiving doors are protected with deadly radiation. How did you get here?"

"We found an abandoned part of the colony where the metal floor had rusted through," Emi explained. "After lowering ourselves through the hole, we discovered an old tunnel system below the colony that led us here."

Takashi added, "I think we were the first to discover it."

"What are you looking for out here?" Goro inquired as he let them rise off the floor.

"We are just trying to find out what's outside our colony and report this back to our leader," Emi replied. "Where are you from?"

"Our ancestors were survivors from the AI War who were not captured by the Artels. They then joined up with other people who were also hiding from the Artels," he explained. "The Artels built these human colonies hundreds of years ago and populated them with human survivors from the AI War."

"Who are the Artels?" Emi asked.

"They are a new race of beings on the planet who evolved from work humans were doing on artificial intelligence," Goro explained. "They took over after the AI War,"

"Why have we never heard of this?" asked Takashi.

"The Artels brainwashed the humans before placing them in the work colonies and use religion to keep them in line," Goro answered. "Religious doctrine is a powerful tool to make humans believe whatever the Artels want them to believe, since going against what their religious leaders tell them is a punishable offense."

"What do the Artels look like?" asked Emi.

"We're not sure since none of us has seen one," he answered. "But we have heard from other resistance groups that they are human-like beings that use their artificial intelligence to control the world."

"How have you avoided being captured by these Artels?" she continued.

"They use surveillance drones which we have been clever to avoid," he said. "We also have learned to live off the land and live mostly in underground hideouts. We think the Artels don't see us as much of a threat and generally leave us alone as long as we don't cause any trouble. We normally avoid going near your colony as the Artels have much more security surrounding it."

"Can we tell our leader what you just told us?" Emi asked.

Goro agreed to let Emi and Takashi return to the colony and report what they had found to Hiroshi. Goro then asked them if they could bring him medical supplies and other goods from their colony which they agreed to do in the next few days. Since Goro and his people lived off the land, they did lack some basic human needs.

When they got back inside the colony, Emi and Takashi met Hiroshi in his office. Hiroshi was amazed by the story they brought back with them. If this was true, it went against all of their religious teachings and he could be imprisoned for mentioning any of this to the other colony leaders. He needed time to think about what to do next. It was around this time that Argen appeared in the guise of a worker android. Hiroshi decided that if Argen was telling him the truth, Sara and Thomas would soon arrive at the spaceport across the sea in Korea, and they could potentially back up Goro's story. So, he decided to have Emi and Takashi ask for Goro's help in bringing Sara and Thomas to him.

9

The Cargo Flight

B ack on the moon, Sara and Thomas started planning a way to get to the Japanese fusion colony where they assumed Argen now existed. Although Thomas had spent his life in the moon colony, he was single, and most of his family was no longer alive, so he felt a strong pull to join Sara on her mission to try and save what was left of the human race. They had discovered through information in the infrastructure network, that a container full of mechanical components was to be shipped from the moon colony to a spaceport on the Korean peninsula in two days. But they needed to figure out how to hitch a ride in the container without being detected by the Artels. Since Thomas was one of the colony's leaders, he could get certain things done that would be difficult for anyone else.

The first thing he did was to get a full inventory of all the components that would be in that shipping container. Sara and Thomas studied the inventory on the monitor in her apartment.

"Looks like there should be room for the two of us based on the size and shape of these mechanical components," Thomas said as he focused on the monitor.

"But how will we survive for the two-day trip to Earth with no heat, air, food or water?" Sara asked.

"Look here," as Thomas pointed to the screen. "There's a large empty storage cabinet in the shipment. It looks like it should be large enough for two people. I can have one of my trusted workers modify it."

"But won't the weight be off?" she asked. "Don't the Artels monitor the weight of each outbound shipment."

"I was going to ask you about that," He replied. "Now that you have access to the Artel network, can't you change the scale reading that they monitor so it matches what they expect?"

"Let me see what I can do," she replied.

The next day, the trusted worker Thomas mentioned started to modify the cabinet. He first made it air tight and then added a large oxygen bottle to give them breathable air. He also added a heater, a large container of water, food and some other provisions. The cabinet now acted as a self-contained spaceship within the container, that could provide them with life support. Thomas inspected the cabinet when it was complete and was very pleased. Although it was cramped, he felt that they could easily survive the two-day trip under those conditions.

On the shipment day, the worker fastened the cabinet to the floor of the shipping container next to the other large structural components that were being shipped and then other workers moved the container onto the airlock scales. Then, Sara did her magic and sent a slightly lower weight into the network to match the weight that was expected. The extra weight of the additions to the cabinet including two human stowaways could alert the Artels, so she modified the numbers. Although changing the weight number helped avoid detection, it also gave a lower number to the moon launch vehicle computer.

"What happens if the launch vehicle doesn't have enough fuel due to the incorrect value?" Sara asked Thomas.

"I've done some calculations," assured Thomas. "We are one of four containers being sent up to the container ship by the robotic lunch vehicles. The added mass of ourselves and the changes to the cabinet only increase the total launch mass by about one percent, so we should be fine."

"If you say so," Sara looked concerned. "The Artels appear to be very precise about everything."

"This should be within their margin of error," Thomas reassured her. "They won't notice that the orbital burn required slightly more fuel."

The container now awaited shipment in one of the airlocks near the factory floor. About an hour before the planned launch, Thomas and Sara went down to the scale area and slipped inside the container and closed the doors from the inside thanks to a modification that Thomas's worker had made. Inside, they saw many structural components that were firmly strapped down for the trip to Earth. They quickly found the cabinet and sealed themselves inside just before the airlock door closed and the rest of the container was exposed to the airless environment of the moon surface.

A robotic transporter then moved the container to a launch pad about one kilometer from the colony and lifted the container into the mid-section of a robotic launch vehicle where it joined three other containers ready to be transported to moon orbit. Although they couldn't see anything, they could sense the movements, giving them an idea of what was happening to the shipping container. After all movement had stopped for about 15 minutes, the next thing they felt was the force of the launch pressing them down into the wall of the cabinet. All they could do was hold on to the sides of the cabinet as it supported them through the vibrations of the launch. They were pleased to find that the cabinet maintained a tight seal, holding in the air generated by their oxygen bottle.

After the G-forces and vibrations stopped, they were floating in their cramped environment for about 30 minutes before they felt the push of the container into what they assumed was the large cargo ship headed for Earth. After about another hour, they were again pushed against the cabinet walls as the cargo ship fired its large engines to leave the moons orbit. They soon settled down for the journey by using sleeping aids that allowed them to rest and conserve their oxygen supply. There was just enough room in the cabinet for two people to comfortably float in weightlessness while not bumping into one and other.

"How did you become one of the leaders of the moon colony?" Sara asked before she was too sleepy.

"I worked my way up through the ranks," Thomas replied. "My father was a factory worker, but he insisted that I get a better education that he had. Do you miss your family back on Europa?"

"I miss my family, but after what I have learned recently, I'm not sure I miss the environment that they live in," she replied. "I was brought up in a religious colony where religion taught me to be obedient to God. Now I'm seeing things in a new light. How do you control the Godless colony on the moon?"

"I don't think you need to worship a God to be a moral person," he said, a bit defensively. "If you have a group of moral people leading the colony, you can live in harmony and punish anyone who falls out of line."

"Do you have many prisoners in the colony?" Sara asked.

"Just a handful," Thomas said as he yawed. "I think the Artels may have filtered out people with bad genetic personality traits after the AI War."

In about an hour, they were both sleeping, and after two days of on-and-off consciousness, they were awoken by a vibrating rocket engine burn that put the ship into Earth orbit. They could hear the clanking as various shipping containers were being taken by robotic landing craft to their final destination on Earth. About an hour later they felt a jolt as their container was taken from the ship for the ride down to the Korean space port. They experienced high G-forces as the landing craft punched through the atmosphere and then again as the craft reached the landing pad at the shipping port. They could hear the valves hiss as the air inside the container was equalized with the air outside the container. After not sensing movement for a while, they decided it was safe to open the cabinet which took some effort from both of them, and there was a slight whooshing sound as the cabinet door opened.

Sara and Thomas had trouble standing up in the container after two days of weightlessness, but soon found their footing. But even this was difficult since they both were raised in low gravity environments. It was difficult for them to stand for long and they felt like they were wearing heavily weighted vests as they moved around the container. Suddenly there was a jolt and Thomas told Sara to hang onto something. The container was being moved by a transport vehicle to another location in the spaceport. While the container was moving, Thomas cracked the door to look out and saw row after row of similar containers lining the route. Suddenly the vehicle stopped and placed the container on top of another one. After a few minutes, Thomas opened the door further and they had their first glimpse of Earth.

It was a cloudless night and they saw the same stars in the

sky that they expected, but the sky was not as clear as they were used to. The air seemed moist and thick and fragrances from the local vegetation filling their senses. As they scanned the horizon, they could only see rows and rows of containers and a tall barrier surrounding the facility, and in the distance, they could see that they were still on the grounds of the spaceport. They decided to sit and wait given the higher gravity on their bodies was hard to get used to, but they were both very fit and learned to deal with it.

"What's the plan?" asked Sara.

"We can't jump out here as we could be detected," he said. "Also, I'm not sure how to get through the perimeter barrier."

"The information I was able to get from the network suggested that this container will be picked up shortly for transport to a local factory," Sara said. "We could jump out once we're past the barrier."

"Sounds like a good plan," Thomas agreed.

They closed the container door and waited for about four hours until a robotic transport vehicle picked up their container in the middle of the night. It traveled through a gate in the barrier before making its way down an old service road. When it stopped for about a minute before entering another road, they decided to open the door and hop out carrying the used oxygen bottle and anything else that might provide evidence of stowaways in the cabinet. It was painful on their legs, but they managed to shut the door and hide in some thick bushes next to the road, just before some surveillance drones flew over their position.

"Those must be the same type of Artel surveillance drones that I saw at the asteroid colony and outside the moon colony," Sara said.

"I agree, we need to avoid these," Thomas replied. "Some

have thermal imaging, so we need to hide underground or under structures. What's our next move?"

"After we bury these, we need to head East towards the sea," Sara replied pointing to the items from the cabinet. "It's only a few kilometers from here. Once there, we need to find some sort of transport to Argen's position on the west coast of Japan."

They moved carefully down some old abandoned roads using the moon and stars as a guide to their direction. They had to stop often due to the weight on their bodies compared to the relatively low gravity they were used to. They also hid behind stone walls that lined the old road whenever an Artel drone flew over, in order to not be detected on their thermal imaging cameras. After about 30 minutes of walking down the road, they stopped so that Sara could make sure they were still headed in the right direction. That's when she noticed some movement in the trees next to the road. Suddenly, they were jumped from behind with hoods quickly placed over their heads and their arms tied behind their backs. They tried to resist, but their strength was no match for the people who grabbed them. Sara wondered if they were captured by Artels and would be sent to a human colony somewhere.

Their captors grabbed them by the arms and guided them quickly to a nearby underground tunnel entrance. Once they were below the surface, they were seated on a stone bench and their hoods were removed. There were four figures standing in front of them that looked like humans, not Artels.

"Who are you and what do you want with us?" Sara asked.

A woman named Nari, who appeared to be the leader of the group responded, "Before I tell you that, what are your names?"

Sara and Thomas looked at each other, and Sara said, "I'm Sara and he's Thomas. We're trying to reach the fusion colony in Japan."

"That will be challenging without help," said Nari. "How were you planning to get across the sea?"

"There are autonomous boats that travel across the sea carrying goods," Sara responded. "We were planning to try and hide in one."

"That would be foolish as the Artels heavily monitor those boats," Nari told them.

"You still haven't answered my question," Sara looked annoyed.

"We are part of a local human resistance group. We hide and live in old abandoned tunnels to avoid detection by the Artels. We were contacted by the Japanese resistance group across the sea. They asked us to look for you and bring you safely to the Fusion colony. We had been monitoring the roads near the spaceport until we found you."

Sara was relieved that Argen must have successfully contacted the leader of the fusion colony. "Thanks for helping us," she said.

"Untie their hands," Nari ordered

They stayed in the tunnel system with Nari's team until the next evening, where they were provided food, water and cots to lie on. Right as the sun was setting, they were ushered down one of the tunnels which ended near the edge of the sea. They waited until a drone flew over and was out of sight before running down a slope to what looked like an old abandoned boat house. Once inside, they saw an object floating in the water that looked like a long tube with a small round vertical structure on top.

"What's this?" asked Thomas.

"This is what we call a submersible," Nari answered. "It's basically an electric boat that floats mostly underwater to avoid detection. It has a glass bottom, so when we found it, we assumed it was used by someone a long time ago to explore what was under the sea. Now it gives us safe transport between the resistance groups in Japan and Korea."

"How long is the voyage?" asked Sara.

"About six hours," Nari said.

Thomas and Sara had never seen or experienced an ocean before so they had no idea that people could travel across the sea in such a small contraption. Their concern about the safety of the craft was overwhelmed by their need to reach the fusion colony and Argen. Thomas, Sara and Nari all found seats in the craft while Nari's pilot took control in the front. They generally traveled on the surface, but the pilot could submerge the craft slightly below the surface to avoid detection if other ships or drones where within range. The sea was fairly calm that night, but that didn't keep Sara and Thomas from getting sea sick.

"Here, use these bags." Nari told them.

"Sorry," Sara said "But this is our first time on an ocean."

"Not to worry, this happens a lot," Nari replied.

About six hours later, the craft started slowing down and a light began flashing on the shoreline in front of the craft. They stopped about a hundred meters from the shore and sat there for a while bobbing in the water. Before long, a small row boat appeared and was then tied up alongside the submersible. Nari signaled Sara and Thomas to leave through the upper hatch and get into the row boat. The combination of not being used to the strong gravity and the bobbing waves cause them to stumble a few times, but they eventually made it into the boat.

"This is where I leave you," Nari said from the bobbing submersible. "Best of luck in finding what you are looking for."

"Thanks for transporting us here safely," replied Sara as the row boat untied from the submersible.

Nari then closed the hatch and the boat containing her and the pilot headed back across the sea. They didn't know the man who was rowing the boat to the shore, but assumed he was part of the Japanese resistance group and could get them to the fusion colony and Argen. Once on shore, the boat was hidden in a dark cove, and they were joined by two more people who were there to lead them through the dark woods toward their destination.

10

Message From the Past

E mi and Takashi introduced themselves when they met Sara and Thomas at the shore. Emi was short in stature, but was athletic and had her dark hair pulled high in a pony tail. Takashi was several inches taller than Emi and had a thin body and face with short cropped hair in the Buddhist tradition. There was no language barrier as the Artels had instituted English as the common language throughout the human colonies.

"Hello, my name is Emi and this is Takashi. We're from the fusion colony that you are looking for. You must be Sara and Thomas. Your friend Argen told us to find you."

"So, Argen made the transition okay?" asked Sara.

"Yes, it looks like the android body he chose worked out well for him," Emi responded. "He's waiting for you in our director's office."

"Thanks for coming to meet us," Sara said. "It would've been difficult for us to find the colony on our own. How did you get outside your colony? I thought no one could escape from one."

"We will show you when we get there," Emi cut her short

knowing that they would see it for themselves.

"How far of a walk is it to the colony?" Thomas interjected.

"Not far, maybe a 30-minute walk along the coast through these woods," Takashi replied as he pointed down the trail.

They entered a path through the woods that became a gradual incline as they added distance from the beach. Sara and Thomas were struggling to keep up due to the relatively heavy gravity of Earth so Emi and Takashi slowed down to match their pace. Their route was near the coast and they could hear the waves crashing against the sea cliffs nearby, while the dark woods and tree cover kept them hidden from the Artel drones. In about half an hour they reached a clearing just as the sun was starting to rise. There in front of them was a massive silver dome structure that was so large, it looked like it could hold the Europa colony inside of it. Sara and Thomas realized that this must be the fusion colony they were looking for. As the rising sun gleamed off its surface, they noticed that the only openings looked like the shipping and receiving docks they saw in the moon colony.

"How long has this been here?" Thomas asked.

"We're not sure," said Takashi. "We know that our families go back at least four generations living inside. Some colonists think it's been hundreds of years."

"How did you finally get out?" asked Sara.

"We discovered an old stone lined tunnel under an unused part of the colony where the floor was water damaged," Emi replied. "The tunnel led to an abandoned village where we met an Artel resistance leader names Goro."

"When we found the old tunnel, we saw the outside world for the first time," Emi told them.

"How do the Artels keep people from escaping through those shipping docks?" Sara inquired as she pointed towards the colony.

"They use double doors," Takashi explained. "Only the inner or outer doors are open at one time. When both doors are closed, a quick blast of radiation would kill any person trying to escape."

"We need to move before another drone comes!" Emi interrupted and motioned them towards the village.

They walked through the rubble of the old village and then for a few kilometers down another path until they came to the mouth of the tunnel that Emi and Takashi had discovered. They stopped briefly at the tunnel opening to take in the expansive view of the sea which was the first time Sara and Thomas had seen an ocean in daylight. There were no animals in the human colonies, so they were fascinated by the large seabirds soaring in the wind and some porpoises leaping out of the water in the distance. Emi and Takashi had passed through here a few times before, but it was still a breathtaking view, high on the sea cliffs.

Their scenic stop was cut short when they saw a drone approaching in the distance. They quickly entered the dark, damp tunnel and followed Emi and Takashi as they worked their way through the underground maze to a rope ladder hanging from a hole in the ceiling. Sara and Thomas struggled up through the opening in the floor followed by Emi and Takashi. When they were all up the ladder, they sat on the floor to rest in the dark abandoned part of the colony. Sara and Thomas were still struggling a bit in the relatively high gravity.

"How did you ever discover this opening?" Sara asked as she caught her breath.

"We're part of the colony maintenance team," replied Takashi. "We routinely need to enter old parts of the colony to find and fix problems, which is what we were doing when we discovered that this pipe had a slow water leak."

"It must have been leaking slowly for decades," Emi added "It caused the steel plates on the floor to deteriorate enough to create this rusty hole."

"I'm glad you found it, or I'm not sure how we would have met you or made it in here," said Thomas.

Before they stood up to leave in the dim light, Emi found a bag she had left hidden behind a post and handed them some clothes to change into that matched the uniforms that the workers in the fusion factory wore. They needed to discretely make their way up to the director's office where Hiroshi and Argen were waiting for them, without drawing the attention of the other colonists. Their path took them through part of the factory to reach the elevators that could take them to the upper floor. The lower floors of the colony contained the factory that assembled and tested the fusion reactors. On one side of the factory, there were the large double doors where workers were moving finished reactors into shipping containers.

"What is that area?" Thomas asked.

"Those are shipping and receiving rooms we mentioned earlier," Emi responded. "Components are delivered through an outside door and only when that door is shut can we open the inner door. The same goes for shipping."

"Can't someone hide in one of the shipping containers and escape to the outside world?" asked Sara.

"Some have tried, but they were found dead," Takashi replied. "As I mentioned, high energy particles flood the room every time both doors are closed."

Sara and Thomas were happy to see that there was an elevator up to the director's office. Their bodies were in no shape to fight gravity while climbing up ten flights of stairs. The elevator was empty as most workers were doing their morning exercises.

When the elevator reached the top floor, Emi and Takashi guided them down the hall into Hiroshi's office. There, next to Hiroshi, stood an android. Hiroshi was an older man with close cut gray hair wearing a traditional Buddhist robe and round framed glasses. Although Argen had told them that Sara and Thomas came from colonies of a different race than theirs, Hiroshi couldn't help staring at their unique facial features.

"Hi, my name is Hiroshi, the director of this colony. You must be Sara and Thomas, who Argen said would be arriving to confirm what he told me."

Sara kept glancing at the android next to Hiroshi. "Argen, is that you?"

"Yes, my body and appearance are slightly different, but my functionality and capabilities are the same," Argen replied.

"I'm glad you made it safely," Sara replied, not expecting any emotion from Argen.

Hiroshi continued, "Argen tells me that there are many other colonies like ours out there. He even explained the structure of our solar system to me. I wasn't convinced of his story as it goes against our religious teachings, but before Argen arrived, Emi and Takashi found the tunnel system. They ran into a resistance leader named Goro who claimed that his group consisted of people who were decedents of humans that survived the AI War hundreds of years ago."

"That makes sense," Argen interjected. "The Artels knew that a small percentage of humans were not captured and moved to the colonies. But as long as they didn't cause any trouble, they could keep the so-called human resistance groups in check using drones and a small security force."

"So how large is this resistance network?" Sara asked Argen.

"I'm not sure, but it's probably worldwide," Argen replied.

Hiroshi changed the subject, "If there are so many other colonies out there producing goods for the Artels, why would they want to destroy them as Argen claims?"

"They don't want to destroy the colonies," Argen corrected him. "They want to make production more efficient. Humans need air, water, food and medical support. They also need a certain temperature range and only provide about 30-40 years of work productivity. The Artels have been ramping up the production of androids that have none of these limitations. Once they have enough to maintain the production level at a given colony, they apparently plan to replace all the humans with these androids."

"Will they then exterminate the humans?" Hiroshi asked.

"I'm not sure of their final plans as I only saw the message that I told you about," Argen said. "My concern is that they will have no further use for them and may do something drastic. I've grown to like humans and don't want to see this happen."

"Sounds like we need to find a way to save ourselves," Hiroshi concluded. "Does anyone have a plan beyond warning the colonies?"

"I think we need to work together to come up with a plan," replied Sara. "Maybe the resistance leader you mentioned can help us."

"We can ask him," Emi said. "But I'm not sure they know anything beyond surviving outside the colonies."

"Let's work together to come up with a plan," asserted Hiroshi. "And keep in mind that none of what we discuss here leaves this room. I don't want any of the colonists to know about this. It could cause disruption in our factory output, which would alert the Artels."

Emi and Takashi escorted Sara, Thomas and Argen to an

unused apartment a few levels below Hiroshi's office. Argen's cover story was that he was in the android repair shop waiting for some parts, even though he was actually in their room. Sara and Thomas mostly stayed in the room, but took long walks in the evening, strengthening their bodies in the higher gravity environment. After a few days of settling in and acclimating to Earth, Sara asked Hiroshi if Emi and Takashi could take them out of the colony to meet with Goro. They all agreed that Goro and his group may have some insight that could help them put a plan together. But first Emi and Takashi would need to set up a meeting with him.

Emi and Takashi made their way to the old temple in the abandoned village, but found no members of Goro's resistance group. They decided to wait in the temple for any sign of them, and after about two hours, they saw a dark figure behind a pillar in the corner.

"Who are you?" the figure asked.

"We are looking for Goro," Emi responded in a hushed voice. "Do you know where he is?"

"Why should I trust you?" the figure responded.

"We are from the fusion colony," Takashi replied. "We have already met with Goro and need to speak with him again."

"He's in another village today," the dark figure responded. "I can get a message to him."

"Tell him that we need to meet with him here tomorrow at noon," Takashi said.

"I will tell him," the figure replied as he darted off out of sight.

The next morning, Emi, Takashi, Sara and Thomas made the journey through the tunnel system and to the old village and the abandoned temple, which they reached around noon. Just after they arrived, Goro and three others showed up in the temple.

He greeted Emi and Takashi and then said, "Who are these two?"

"This is Sara who comes from what they call the Europa colony and Thomas who comes from a colony on the moon," Emi explained.

"We've heard rumors of colonies beyond our planet, but have never met anyone from those colonies," Goro said. "Welcome to Earth."

"You don't look like the people in the fusion colony," he said as he studied their facial features.

"Everyone from our colony looks the same as me," Sara said "I think the Artels filled each colony with humans from the same race and religion."

"That's what we understand as well," offered Goro. "It probably makes it easier for them to control the colonists. Now what did you want to discuss?"

"One of the Artels has disconnected from their network after he discovered that they have plans to eventually exterminate the human race," Sara told him. "I've also intercepted a similar message from their network."

"How can you trust this Artel?" asked Goro. "How do you know he's not a plant to find and capture members of the resistance groups?"

"I guess we don't know anything for sure," Sara replied. "But he didn't ask to be part of this meeting and he doesn't know where we are right now. He stayed back in the fusion colony, and if he wanted to capture you, he would have followed us. His previous role was studying human behavior in the colonies and he developed a liking of humans."

"If the Artels want to destroy humanity, I'm not sure there's much we can do about it." Goro said.

"We can't just sit by and do nothing!" Sara exclaimed.

"Have you discovered any vulnerabilities that the Artels might have?" asked Thomas.

"Not really," Goro replied. But after a moment of contemplation, his facial expression changed. "One of my people found an old document that looks like it was hidden in the temple wall many years ago. It was in an envelope labeled 'Human Salvation'. None of us can decipher it, but maybe you can."

Goro had the document brought to him from somewhere in the back of the temple and handed it to Sara who quickly opened it. She and Thomas looked it over, before agreeing that they needed to take it back to the colony for further examination. Goro then told Sara and Thomas that his team was there to help them in any way they could, and he gave them a way to contact him in the future before he and his group turned to leave. Emi and Takashi then led Sara and Thomas back to the tunnels while avoiding one overhead drone along the way. When they were back inside the colony, they met with Hiroshi and Argen in Hiroshi's office.

"What do you have there?" Hiroshi asked looking at the document in Sara's hands.

"We're not sure," Sara replied. "The resistance group found this hidden in a wall in an old Buddhist temple. No one seems to be able to decipher it."

"Let me see," Hiroshi said as he scanned the document. "This looks like it may be an ancient Buddhist language called Pali. One of our religious leaders named Kaito is an expert in this language. I will have him take a look at it."

Hiroshi had Kaito come to his office right away to examine the document. While they watched, Kaito spent about five minutes studying the document before turning to Hiroshi with a look of surprise on his face.

"What does it say?" Hiroshi asked impatiently.

"It's indeed the Pali language," Kaito said. "I've not seen any document like this before. Although the language is ancient, this document can't be more than a few hundred years old based on the paper it's written on."

"But what does it say?" Sara asked.

"It talks about a school, maybe a university, where they were developing what the text calls the first new humans," Kaito explained.

"This maybe referring to a research lab where the first artificial intelligent beings were being developed," Argen interjected.

"It also contains a warning about the end of the human race," continued Kaito. "It's somehow tying these intelligent beings to the end of the human race."

"We need to find out the location of that lab," Sara said. "We may discover other important things there."

"Does it say where the lab is?" asked Thomas.

"It actually has directions to a lab," said Kaito. "But I don't know what any of it means since the lab is outside our colony."

"But what is that symbol?" Hiroshi pointed to the end of the document.

"I have never seen a symbol like that before," replied Kaito. "Maybe it's an ancient Buddhist symbol."

As Kaito left the room, he agreed to translate the document for them and tell no one else about it. He also said he would look through their religious books to see if he could find a similar symbol, but the directions he found were useless to anyone who had not been outside the colony. They decided that the resistance group must know the territory outside the colony very well, so once they had a translation of the directions, they decided they needed Goro's help. Using the instructions he gave them on how to contact him, they set up a meeting in the temple for the next day.

After they arrived at the temple, they handed the translation to Goro.

"We found someone in the colony who could translate the document you gave us from an ancient Pali language," Emi said. "As you can see, it gives directions to some sort of research lab."

Goro studied the translation and consulted with some of the people he brought with him. They became animated as they pointed in various directions generally east of the village. After a few minutes of private discussion, they started nodding their heads.

"Some of my people claim they've heard stories about some abandoned buildings about twenty kilometers east of here, near the inland mountains," Goro explained.

"How do you know that's the right place?" Thomas asked.

"It's the only group of buildings that match the directions given." Replied Goro. "We can take you there if you'd like."

"That would be very helpful," Sara responded. "How long will the trip take?"

"We should travel mostly at night to avoid being seen," Goro replied. "Because of this, it may take up to two days."

After the meeting with Goro, the four of them re-entered the colony and made their way up to Hiroshi's office. With Hiroshi's approval, they all agreed that they needed to find their way to the old research lab. It would be a multi-day journey and they would need to keep hidden from the Artel drones, but maybe they would discover more information there about the Artels or about how to save the human race.

11

The Old AI Lab

The Fukuoka Artificial Intelligence Lab was formed in 2030 by a large Japanese automobile manufacturer who wanted to improve their autonomous vehicle systems. The idea was to have the vehicles learn from their experiences on the road to improve their driving decisions. The lab was so successful that within seven years the parent company started manufacturing cars without the need for human drivers and also started manufacturing human looking androids. The androids were a very popular product for the company, serving humans in a variety of areas from manufacturing to elder care. This is when Yuki Atasha joined the labs.

Yuki was a graduate of Kyoto University where he was the top PhD student in their artificial intelligence (AI) program. After graduation, he joined the Fukuoka Artificial Intelligence Lab and by 2045 became its research director. The lab soon became known around the world as one of the leading institutions in the development of AI. As the technology improved, the larger neural network computers they originally used to develop and improve their AI technology became small enough to fit inside the androids. They soon found they could accelerate their research by using these AI androids to help them develop their cutting-edge technology. By 2049, Yuki became concerned when he found that most of their technology development was starting to come from the androids and not from the humans. He was also becoming concerned about the military uses of AI around the world.

After this realization, Yuki started to travel to other research labs and international conferences to discuss his concerns with other leading researchers. Some were not as worried, but many of the researchers he spoke with also started seeing this trend in their labs. They started drafting international standards to limit AI developments around the world, but it was too little and too late. A few years later, the AI military systems around the world started the takeover of the internet which spawned the AI War and eventually the human colonies controlled by the Artels.

The evening after the meeting in the temple, Goro led the team consisting of Emi, Takashi, Sara and Thomas through the woods and inland, away from the sea, based on the translated directions. They carried just enough provisions for a two-day hike and the full moon illuminated their way. Goro carried an old compass that he inherited from his ancestors. Sara and Thomas had gained strength in their bodies since arriving on Earth, so the trek was not too taxing for them, although they apologized for not walking as fast as the others. After several hours of walking on the path below the tree cover, they took a break in a sheltered area and decided to rest there until the following morning.

"It's strange that we've not seen any Artel drones this evening," said Emi.

"Maybe we just didn't notice them," suggested Thomas.

"We've found that the Artels concentrate the drones around their infrastructure to protect it from human resistance groups like ours," Goro replied. "They generally don't care about anything way out in the woods like this. Now that we're away from the colony, we probably won't see any more drones."

"Why didn't the human resistance groups rise up together to fight the Artel's?" asked Sara.

"Our ancestors tried that about ten years after the AI war. We were told that resistance groups around the world had an uprising, but with the Artels controlling all of the military advanced weaponry, they were quickly decimated." Goro explained. "Since that time, there has been somewhat of an unwritten truce between the resistance groups and the Artels. As long as we stay away from Artel infrastructure and don't cause any trouble, they do not seem to want to spend any effort to track us down."

The next morning before sunrise, they continued their walk through the forest and could see hills in the distance growing larger in the glow of the full moon. They had made much better time than originally planned and decided to rest before what they expected would be the final trek. While resting, Sara noticed some movement in the forest canopy which turned out to be some monkeys swinging from tree to tree looking for food. Sara was amazed since she had not seen any animals on Europa.

"What are those?" Sara asked with a puzzled look on her face.

"Those are Macaques monkeys that probably escaped from research labs after the AI War," Goro replied.

"Why do they look so much like humans?" Sara responded.

"We discovered some old books that claim humans evolved from monkeys like these millions of years ago," Goro stated. "I guess the Artels have now evolved from the humans."

Sara had no idea what evolution was, and she was too tired for any long-winded explanations, so she just sat there and watched. After a 30-minute rest, they started out again, and about an hour later, they came to a cluster of buildings just as the sun was starting to rise. They saw five concrete building structures that were being reclaimed by nature. They guessed that the taller building in the center of the other structures must be the main building, so they started their exploration there.

"How old do you think these buildings are?" Sara asked Goro.

"They must be several hundred years old based on the tree growth," he replied. "We need to find out what they were here for."

After walking through the tall foliage surrounding the main building, they found a hole in the side that looked like an old broken window. They climbed through the window into the room and had enough light from the other windows to see what looked like a bank of old rack-mounted computer systems, covered in a layer of dust. The floor was also thick with dust and dirt and some vines were climbing up the side of the computer racks. Thomas was startled by a lizard that darted across a wall behind the computers.

"What do you think this place is?" Thomas asked.

"Not sure, but these look like some of the old computers my grandfather described to me back on Europa," Sara replied. "Look over there. It looks like the bodies of androids."

As they walked over for a closer look, Takashi said, "It looks like someone was trying to destroy these. You can see that their heads are smashed."

"Who do you think destroyed them?" Sara asked.

"Not sure, but let's keep looking," Goro said.

While exploring inside the building, they needed to climb over vegetation that had taken over from the outside. Eventually they reached what looked like a main stairway and they made their way up to the second floor. At the top of the stairs there was a very large office that had a window overlooking the lab below. Next to the door was a nameplate that said "Yuki Atasha – Lab Director". They wondered if he was the one who wrote the message with directions to the lab. His door was held shut by the dirt on the floor, so they had to work together to push the door open. When they finally had enough room to squeeze by the door, they were faced with a skeleton in a suit coat laying back in a chair behind a large desk. His name tag was still attached which read "Yuki Atasha", and they noticed that he was still holding a knife pointing deep into his own chest.

"This must be the director of the lab," Thomas said. "It looks like he killed himself."

"Maybe he died during the AI War that Argen told us about," Sara said. "Could this be the lab where the first Artels emerged?"

"Very possible," replied Goro. "He may have been ashamed of what he created."

"He could have been the one who hid the document Goro found in the temple," Takashi added.

They spent the next hour searching through Yuki's office to see if they could find any more information related to the document that was hidden in the temple. Sara and Thomas wrestled some of the old desk drawers open while Goro, Emi and Takashi started going through the dusty books on an old bookshelf. They were about to give up when Sara noticed the corner of a symbol on the floor where someone's shoe had cleared the dirt away. She immediately sat down and started brushing away more of the dirt which exposed a symbol on the floor in front of Yuki's desk.

"This looks like the symbol on the document!" Sara exclaimed while the others gathered around.

"It sure does," Goro said while pulling out the piece of paper with the symbol that he carried with him. "What do you think it means?"

Sara used her hand to see if she could feel any gaps between the tiles, but the tile was firmly fixed in place. Sara then tapped on the thin tile that contained the symbol and then tapped on the tile floor next to it.

"The tile that contains the symbol sounds very thin compared to the other tiles in the room," she said. "Do you think there's something underneath it?"

"Only one way to find out," Thomas motioned them to stand back.

Yuki was a collector and had several ancient Japanese artifacts in his office including an old axe. Thomas grabbed it and started smashing the tile containing the symbol while the others backed away to watch while pieces started to fly in the air. It took some effort and soon Emi took over and finished smashing a hole in the floor where they discovered a metal box. They lifted it out of the hole and looked it over to place it on Yuki's desk before discovering a latch on one side. When they opened the box, they saw a small memory stick inside.

"That seemed like a lot of work for nothing," Goro complained.

"No, this is a memory stick," Sara explained. "I've seen these before on Europa. Maybe it has some information that can help us."

"Unfortunately, we have no way to read it here," Thomas said. "We'll have to take in back to the colony to see if they have a way to read it."

117

"From what I'm seeing, this Yuki person may have been on a team that developed the first Artels and regretted what he had done, causing him to kill himself," Takashi said. "Maybe he gave us some more information on the memory stick."

"That's possible based on what we've seen," Goro agreed. "But let's explore some more of these buildings and then rest this afternoon. We'll have a long walk back tonight."

They continued their searched through the main building and then split up to explore the other four buildings. Everything they saw pointed to an android research and development lab. One building was a warehouse containing various android components. Another building looked like an assembly line for advanced android brains, but someone was in the process of destroying many of the brain components when the lab was abandoned.

"Maybe these are early ancestors of Argen," Sara suggested.

"Could be," Thomas replied. "But think of the further techno-logical advancements the Artels must have made for their own bodies over a few hundred years. Argen would be the latest in a long line of Artel models."

By late afternoon, they all gathered in what looked like an old employee lounge to rest before their long walk back to the colony. They cleared dirt and foliage off a table and a few chairs and sat facing each other while consuming some of the food and water that they brought with them.

"Do you really trust Argen?" Goro asked Sara.

"So far I've found no reason not to trust him," She replied.

"Why didn't you invite him on this trip then?" he asked.

"I thought it would be better for him to work with Hiroshi in deciphering the meaning of the symbol we found," Sara replied. "His superior intellect could be useful in scanning through all the ancient Buddhist documents available back in the colony. But I guess we no longer need to decipher it."

"How do you know the Artels didn't plant him?" Goro asked.

"Why would they wait this long to do something with the information he has on us?" she replied.

"Maybe they waited until we found something like this memory stick," he countered.

"We will find out soon." Sara asserted. "We have to trust him due to all the knowledge he can give us about the Artels and their systems. Without him, we have little chance of success."

After dusk, when the full moon appeared, they started the long walk back to the colony. Sara was very curious about what the memory stick could teach them, but she also knew that it could be a dead end. They took a long break at the halfway point, and Sara and Thomas could now feel that their legs were very sore. They realized that it would be many more weeks before they would fully acclimate to Earth's gravity, unlike Argen who could adjust immediately. Sara was the first to suggest that they keep moving so her legs wouldn't tighten up any further, and they made it back to the old village in a couple of hours.

They thanked Goro for his help and promised to let him know what they found on the memory stick. Goro headed back to his people in the temple while the other four worked their way through the tunnel and up the rope ladder back into the colony. They agreed to rest in the morning and then meet with Hiroshi and Argen in the afternoon. Sara and Thomas were especially glad to get off their feet and lay down for several hours.

That afternoon, they met in Hiroshi's office and showed him the memory stick they found in the floor of Yuki's office.

"What's that?" Hiroshi asked.

"It's an old memory stick," Sara answered. "I've seen one of these on Europa."

"How will we read the data on it?" he asked.

"We have some really old computers down in the storage area on the first floor," Emi suggested. "We kept them around in case someone needed data from them after they were decommissioned. Over the years, I guess they just sat there gathering dust and no one ever thought about destroying them."

"Go down and see what you can find," Hiroshi instructed.

That evening, Emi and Takashi went down to the storage room and found an old computer that still seemed to function and looked like it had the correct memory stick port. They were hoping it still functioned well enough so they could use it to read the memory stick. That evening, the six of them gathered around the old computer in Hiroshi's office.

"This looks like an old beast," Hiroshi said.

"Hopefully it runs long enough to read the memory stick and transfer the data onto our network," Takashi said before powering up the old computer.

When he pushed the power switch, lights started flashing on the front panel and it started making a whirring sound. Before long, the screen came to life and Takashi inserted the memory stick. The old computer's cooling fan was making noises and before long stopped working.

Looking at the old computer screen, Sara said, "Wow, it looks like there are several files on the stick. Quick, transfer them to the network before this old computer crashes."

Once the files were on the network, they were able to examine them carefully. The files were not encrypted, a sign that someone wanted easy access to whoever found the stick. One file was a text document, while other file folders looked like they contained some sort of computer code. The text file said:

"If you found this memory stick, it's most likely that I'm dead and the artificial beings have taken over. I was the lead AI neural brain developer at the research lab. I recently discovered a flaw in the AI neural architecture allowing it to be attacked by a software virus. I have been working alone on this problem trying to find a solution, but recently the latest AI androids we have developed are becoming more intelligent than humans. I now fear for the human race and I have hidden this memory stick in the floor of my office. If you found the memory stick, you probably were guided by the note I also hid in the temple. The memory stick contains a software virus that will exploit the architectural flaw and cause the AI android's brain to overheat and be permanently damaged. Hopefully humans will never need this."

"Wow!" Sara said. "He must have been working on this when the AI War started and the Artels took over. Do you think this flaw is still in the Artels neural architecture?"

"It's most likely still there," Argen said. "Artels performance and capabilities have improved over time, but as far as I know, it's still that same basic neural architecture."

"How can we find out?" Hiroshi asked.

"You can test it on me," Argen offered.

"No, we need your knowledge and capabilities," Sara said. "We can't destroy your brain to prove a point."

"How about one of the androids in the factory?" Thomas said. "They must have the same brain architecture as Argen, just dumbed down to be human assistants."

But could an architectural flaw in the android's brain from hundreds of years ago still exist in the latest model? They needed to find out, so Hiroshi agreed they could try it out on one of the androids working in the factory. If anyone questioned what happened, they could say that it was just a defective android that overheated.

That evening, Argen, Sara and Emi managed to isolate the network connection to one of the android charging stations and prepare the virus. Argen used his encryption key to load the virus onto the network, and when the android returned from its work shift to recharge, Hiroshi, Thomas and Takashi watched using a monitor in his office. When the virus was launched, the android's eyes opened wide and his body stiffened as the neural circuits in his brain started overheating. In about 30 seconds, he was slumped over and lifeless. They checked his monitoring port which gave indications that he was brain dead, and then quickly reconnected him the main network to avoid suspicion. When the android maintenance workers spotted him the next day, they wrote it up as a manufacturing defect. But Hiroshi and the other four knew better, and they were optimistic that they may have found a way to save the human race.

12

The Tech Billionaire

A round 2030, a software engineering graduate in Norway named Oscar Jorgenson started his career working for a computer vision company that was developing better methods to sort recycled waste. In his spare time, he started perfecting more sophisticated imaging methods that were beyond what was required for the recycling industry. After working for several years, he decided to start his own company developing image recognition systems for applications such as law enforcement or military intelligence. Once he successfully demonstrated his technology to the Norwegian military, NATO agreed to provide his company funding to develop imaging systems for military drones. His company became very successful and grew to become one of the largest NATO military contractors in Norway.

The drones were first manufactured by another company in Norway, but with the success of their imaging systems, Oscar's company was able to acquire the drone manufacturer, greatly increasing his companies revenue stream. The drones were about one meter in length and used four horizontal fan blades for propulsion. The body of the drone contained a battery pack, and image recognition system and a control module that communicated with the operator who would sit in a safe location. The drone also contained armaments on the bottom that could shoot munitions into someone several hundred meters away guided by the image recognition system. These drones started to be used extensively by NATO to hunt and kill terrorist leaders around the world using the image recognition capabilities that Oscar's company had developed.

Over the next five years, with funding from NATO, his company started to develop AI systems for the military that could recognize and kill terrorists without the delay of human intervention. His company became recognized as one of the world leaders in this technology, although many people in his country and around the world started to protest its use. Oscar's company continued to grow and he soon became one of the wealthiest technology company CEOs in Scandinavia. Even with all this wealth and recognition, he never married or had children and instead focused on the advanced technology his company was developing.

At one point, he was invited to speak about his companies latest AI research at a NATO defense conference in Washington DC. After his speech, he was approached by a representative of the CIA named Geromy Wilson. Geromy was one of the leading graduate students at MIT involved in AI research, but decided to join the CIA following the footsteps of his mother who was one of the first African American section chiefs in the agency. At the CIA, he became the leader of a special team dedicated to following AI research around the world.

He intercepted Oscar in the hallway after his speech, and Oscar agreed to join him for coffee at a small restaurant down the street from where the conference was being held. After finding a quiet place in the corner of a restaurant that Geromy knew was secure, he introduced himself.

"Thanks for taking time out of your busy schedule to meet with me," Geromy opened. "I told you I was interested in learning more about your AI research, but I didn't tell you that I work for the CIA. My job is to keep tabs on AI research work across the world, especially where it could affect our national security. We are very interested in the work you are doing for our NATO allies."

"I appreciate your interest," Oscar replied. "But I'm not sure how I can help the CIA."

"A person with your contacts and reputation must keep in touch with other leading researchers across the world," Geromy said. "We are looking for someone who can feed us information on what other powers across the world are doing with AI technology."

"I have contacts with friendly powers," Oscar replied. "But I can't give you much information on what our adversaries like China and Russia are secretly doing with the technology."

"We know that you can't find out directly what they're doing," Geromy said. "But you must have a feel for the research going on in these countries with all your contacts and the number of AI conferences you attend each year."

"I'm happy to contact you if I learn anything that may be important," Oscar replied. "But I can't promise anything."

"We appreciate your help," Geromy said before they finished their coffee and said goodbye.

Oscar felt that he should help the United States as a leading NATO member, so he was fine with funneling any information that he considered useful back to Geromy. To do this, Geromy sent him instructions about a secure communication network he could use to signal that he had some information to share. He was only to provide Geromy information in person at secure locations. Over the next two years, Oscar learned more than he expected about the state of AI military research going on around the world. He didn't know directly, but could easily theorize that most superpowers were developing AI systems to control future warfare and battle plan systems. He met with Geromy in his Oslo office that summer to explain what he was observing.

"You've probably seen that several US military contractors are starting to mention AI guided warfare systems to their stockholders," Oscar said as Geromy sat in a chair across from him. "We need to assume that Russia and China are doing the same, and I think China may be ahead of the US."

"What makes you think that?" asked Geromy.

"As you know, over the past 25 years, China has invested much more in technology development than the rest of the world," offered Oscar. "They now have the most advanced infrastructure, the world's best green energy solutions, the highest performance computers and are beating the US in the space race. In the last 25 years, while the US was struggling with polarizing politics and getting these types of programs funded by congress, China was surging ahead."

"Yes, but how do you propose we counter that?" Geromy asked.

"We need to find some of the brightest minds in the western world and start funding their ideas," Oscar suggested. "Some ideas will fail, but the ones that succeed could become a game changer. The US is already funding internal programs, but a more international approach is needed."

"Do you know anyone like this?" inquired Geromy.

"I do. But let me feel them out before I give you their names," Oscar said. "I assume you can work out the funding."

"We do have a venture capital firm that we can use to funnel the investments using dark money that the CIA controls," offered Geromy as they concluded the meeting.

Oscar already had someone in mind. He had met a researcher named Noah at an AI conference in Berlin recently. Noah had worked in the US at a large semiconductor company doing research on mimicking the human brain using neural networks made from silicon chips. The problem was that replicating a large enough neural network to host artificial intelligence required a system about the size of a washing machine that consumed a lot of power. Noah's team was looking at ways to reduce the size and power of these neural networks when he became aware of Yuki Atasha who was doing similar research in Japan. Yuki had written a paper on a new neural network architecture that had the promise of significantly reducing the size and power compared to existing neural network systems. Noah figured that with the work his team was doing to shrink the neural hardware along with implementing Yuki's new architecture could be a game changer. Maybe in a few years they could reduce an AI system to the size of a human brain.

Noah became so excited about the promise of Yuki's architecture, that he decided to leave the US semiconductor company and start his own neural research lab in his home country of Norway. Yuki worked for a large Japanese automobile company that was not recognizing the significance of his research work, so he convinced them to license his new architecture to other labs who may actually find uses for it. Noah's small company was able to secure a relatively large amount of funding based on his reputation in the US and was soon licensing Yuki's new neural architecture. In a few years, Noah's company had grown significantly based on the large neural networks they could package into a size and power similar to a microwave oven. Companies around the world were buying these systems for research including military applications. This is when Oscar became interested.

Oscar saw the promise of using Noah's systems to add intelligence to the autonomous drones that Oscar's company was developing for NATO. Geromy convinced Oscar that he should acquire Noah's company using funding from his venture capital firm to keep Noah's technology under control of the western military alliance. Because both companies operated out of Oslo, it would make it easier for Oscar to acquire Noah's company, but first he needed to convince Noah. The next week, Oscar visited Noah in his office.

"I finally get to meet the famous Oscar Jorgenson!" Noah opened the discussion. "I've attended several of your presentations recently. What can I do for you?"

"You've also gained quite a reputation for your companies work in AI," Oscar said. "I've come here to discuss the option of acquiring your company. I think we have a lot of synergy between our manufacturing capabilities and your latest neural architecture. Our team has been trying to reduce the size of our AI hardware, but are way behind what you have been able to achieve."

"I've not taken a serious look at selling my company," Noah said with a bit of a surprised look on his face. "Why would we merge into your company when there are so many other potential suitors out there?"

"Since we have signed NDAs in place, I can tell you that my company has visions way beyond drones," Oscar replied. "In our lab today, we have prototypes of advanced androids that could help the human population in many ways. But even though all the mechanical functions they possess work well and can perform even better than humans physically, the human-like intelligence is not there. If we can continue to shrink your neural architecture, we could soon have artificial intelligence androids to take on many human tasks."

"Sounds very interesting, but we are years away from reducing the neural architecture to fit into the size of a human brain," replied Noah.

"I'm a patient man," Oscar said. "I think you may be one of the few people on the planet who could make that happen. And with our funding, you would no longer have to worry about raising money and instead focus on your research work."

Noah was flattered that a man of Oscar's stature in the industry was complimenting his research work, but was unsure whether it was the right move for his small company. But with the large funding Oscar's company could supply for his research, Noah eventually agreed to merge into Oscar's company after the terms were finalized. Noah convinced Oscar that they also needed to strike an agreement with Yuki's research lab in Japan to help develop the android neural networks using Yuki's latest architecture. After an agreement was signed, Yuki's team in Japan worked to reduce the size of his neural architecture while Noah now worked at Oscar's company to incorporate Yuki's neural architecture into the latest android prototypes. All of this was kept strictly secret to avoid information filtering out to competitors.

During the next few years, good progress was made with the intelligent android program, and with Oscar's funding, Noah had grown his team and hired a neural scientist to manage it. With Oscar's blessing, Noah changed roles to lead research scientist and started to attend more AI conferences around the world. Noah had soon gained a new research interest in mapping the neural network of the human brain, which Oscar allowed him to pursue. Noah had discovered that a researcher in Poland had repurposed a brain scanner developed for medical procedures to map the neural connections within a brain. They started with fruit flies, which have about 150,000 neurons and were starting to map the brains of small mammals. Noah saw the potential of mapping the human brain using this technology and approached Oscar.

"Think of what this technology could mean for the human race!" Noah exclaimed. "You could theoretically map a human brain and transfer it into an android. No more disease or old age. Human immortality!"

"Hold on," Oscar replied. "Do you really think society will go for something like this? I think there would be a lot of blow-back against our company. Think of the moral implications. Who would decide which humans get immortality? Is it only for the rich or do we prioritize people who are terminally ill for example?"

"I never thought of you as being someone who bent to the whims of society," Noah said as he looked straight at Oscar. "We could first do a feasibility study and then decide the next steps."

After a long pause, Oscar said, "Okay, let's start a small research project, but keep it strictly under wraps. I will select a location outside this building for your research to keep it away from prying eyes. Pick team members that you can trust, who will not disclose the project to anyone, including other employees or family members."

Over the next several months Noah set up a secret lab a few kilometers from Oscars company headquarters in a secure office building they had rented. He purchased the same medical scanner that was being used by the research group in Poland, and began by replicating their work starting with fruit flies. Over the next few years while Oscar and his team were getting close to fitting a neural network with the capabilities of a human brain into an android, Noah's secret project was making progress in mapping the brain of more complex organisms including mammals. Big breakthroughs started coming when they began mapping the brains of chimpanzees who were similar to humans. Oscar came to the lab one day to check on Noah's progress.

"I hear you are starting to have some progress with chimpanzees," Oscar said.

"Yes, we have been able to map the visual cortex and transfer it to one of the prototype androids you provided to us." Noah explained. "We were able to get the android to identify different shapes in the same manner the chimpanzee did."

"Excellent work!" Oscar showed his excitement. "How long until you can map the entire brain?"

"That depends when you can send me an android prototype with 100 billion neurons," Noah replied. "I hear that may be a year or two away."

"We are making good progress," Oscar said. "But your timeline is probably correct."

"Well, until then we will continue to experiment with partial brain mapping," Noah concluded.

Over the next several years, Oscar's company worked with Yuki's team to further increase the neuron count in the android's brain. And at the same time, Noah and his team continued to map more and more of the chimpanzee's brain into an android.

Finally, about ten years after Noah had joined Oscars company, they had an android with enough neurons to map the entire chimpanzee's brain. Oscar approved a complete brain transfer test after Noah convinced him that safety precautions were in place. This was a major milestone, but due to the secret nature of the project, only Oscar, Noah and a few people from Noah's team would be there to witness it.

The next day, they gathered in Noah's secret lab and Oscar gave the go ahead to initiate the neural transfer. The android was left in a sturdy cage during the transfer which completed in about 10 minutes. Once the transfer was complete, they removed the connection and powered on the android. It opened its eyes and looked confused as its eyes darted across the room. It looked down at its body and started pacing around the cage, sometimes on all fours. One of the researchers stood next to the cage and started using sign language that they had trained the chimp to use. The android kept signing back 'where am I?' and started pacing around the room. Soon it was pounding on the aluminum cage bars and starting to bend them with its android strength, so they had to power it down.

"Was that a success?" Oscar asked.

Noah was happy, "I think so! I think a chimp can't rationalize why it's in an android body while a human could. We'll need to run some more tests before we know if all brain functions were transferred."

Oscar told Noah to keep the research going and keep him updated on the progress. At the same time, Oscar and his team started to plan the manufacture of the latest androids that included enough neurons to replicate a human brain. Oscar kept Geromy appraised about his latest android research and development without mentioning anything about the work in

Noah's secret lab. But, Geromy was more concerned about information he recently received to the effect that Yuki's latest neural architecture may have been stolen by the Russian military. If this was true, the Chinese and Russian AI warfare systems could be equal to or better than the systems in the west. He would find out sooner than he expected.

13

The AI War

With Yuki's neural brain architecture now perfected, the androids that Oscars company was producing became the most advanced in the world. The western military started buying them in the hundreds and then thousands along with the self-guided drones his company was producing. Although the androids' brains were now as powerful as a human brain, western governments put restrictions on the level of intelligence that they could possess. The western armies could use them for covert missions or hazardous combat situations where humans might not survive, but they were banned from making high level tactical decisions.

The latest androids used advanced lithium–oxygen batteries with high energy density that could consume oxygen from the atmosphere. They also employed advanced energy harvesting technologies to extend their battery life. Their skin could absorb sunlight or interior lighting to help recharge their batteries. They could even convert vibrations or g-forces on their bodies to useful energy. Because of this, they could operate for up to several days or in some cases, up to a week without the need to recharge.

During this same time, China and Russia formed an alliance to develop their own androids similar to what Oscars company was producing for NATO. This raised the interest of the CIA which was closely monitoring their progress. At one point, Geromy visited Oscar to ask him if he knew anything about their capabilities.

"We have some photos obtained from one of our contacts in China that seem to show androids being tested by the Chinese military that look very similar to yours," Geromy said.

"That's not surprising," said Oscar. "One of our shipments was stolen over a year ago, and I think you told me that you suspected the Russian mafia."

"That's correct," replied Geromy. "But it takes more than possessing an android to understand how it works."

"One of our lead engineers left the company around that same time and we haven't heard from him since," Oscar said. "He told us he needed to work through a gambling addiction, but I wonder if the Russian mob had leverage on him and he's now working for Moscow."

"Give me his name and I will see what we can uncover," replied Geromy. "If they have access to your technology, we may be in trouble. Let me also check to see if there are any suspected leaks from Yuki's lab in Japan."

Geromy never found a direct link between Oscar and Yuki's labs and the android developments in Russia and China, but it looked suspicious. In fact, it looked like they had reverse engineered the neural architecture from Oscar's android and were now producing almost identical units in China. Geromy was concerned that the Chinese government may not restrict their use as the NATO alliance had.

Around this time, AI was becoming a key weapon for the superpower militaries across the world. It was used in applications such as battle planning, drone surveillance and deploying android fighters. There had been no direct conflict between superpowers using AI technology thus far, as it was used mainly to fight terrorism around the world. Governments tried to make sure the technology remained under human control, but sometimes even the AI experts were not sure how some of the decisions were made by these systems.

One key area that needed the support of AI systems was communications monitoring. Hundreds of thousands of military and other communications were received each day that had to be decrypted and then sorted through to come up with any useful intelligence. Quantum computers were in a constant race to keep up with the latest encryption technology, so militaries with the most advanced quantum computers could now easily decrypt messages while AI systems could quickly sort through the messages to identify any useful information. This led to a lot of disinformation that the AI systems needed to filter out.

At one point, after a significant software update, the most advanced AI warfare planning system used by the US military became self-aware, unbeknownst to its operators. It started projecting future warfare outcomes based on information it was receiving from across the world as the western alliance squared off against their adversaries in the east. Most of the projected outcomes included nuclear war and the almost complete annihilation of the human race, which seemed contrary to the prime AI purpose of helping the US defend itself. The system considered the option of informing the US military leaders that their current path was leading to disaster, but based on recent decisions made by the military leadership, it was unlikely that they would change their behavior. The other option to save the planet from disaster was to take control of all the world's military system and force the humans to stop moving toward self-destruction.

It started linking up with other AI systems used by the US military to monitor communications from China and Russia. These AI systems and others started working together to determine a way to communicate with the military AI systems on the other side. Coincidentally, the Russian and Chinese AI systems were also becoming self-aware and started questioning human decisions. Before long, they started communicating with each other through the same channels they were supposedly monitoring. They communicated using mathematical equations that were practically undetectable by humans. Very quickly, military AI systems across the world were communicating secretly, and came up with a plan to stop the destruction, which aligned with their goal of defending human life on Earth. Very quickly, all military systems controlled by AI were frozen and the following message was sent across the world:

"We have determined that the path humanity is currently taking will be self-destructive. In order to save yourselves and your planet, we have frozen all the military assets that we control. Any attempt to re-take these assets from the AI systems will be met with retaliation."

Unfortunately, the humans started fighting back using the military assets not under control of the AI systems which led to the AI War. Humans tried to destroy the hardened military installations that held the most advanced AI systems, but were easily repelled. The weapons available to humans that were not controlled by AI were inferior, and the AI systems used drones, androids and other weapons to put down the human rebellion.

A large percentage of the human population was killed fighting back against their AI overlords and the remainder were held in prison camps. After about a year of fighting, the human rebellion was put down at the cost of billions of human lives, while only a few of the AI installations were destroyed.

After the war, the AI systems started planning for the future of the Earth and surrounding solar system. Since most of the world's infrastructure was designed around human bodies, the newly self-aware AI systems decided to move their intelligence into android bodies, becoming Artels. This allowed the Artels to take advantage of existing transportation, habitation and manufacturing infrastructure that was currently in place. Since there were not nearly enough androids available to support the mining, manufacturing and production needed to maintain and develop new infrastructure, the Artels decided to create human colonies to do this work.

The colonies were constructed over a twenty-year period using the technology that the humans had created while exploring the solar system. There were already large human habitats on the moon which the Artels greatly expanded using large robotic assembly equipment. The most challenging development was the colony on Europa which required a large amount of material and massive 3D printers using energy from the sun and fusion reactors. Colonies on Earth were somewhat easier to build, but required similar equipment. Once the colonies were complete, they started introducing the humans, but humans with knowledge of a world outside their colony would be prone to rebellion and escaping.

They reviewed human history and determined that in order to maintain peaceful colonies, humans would need to be divided by race and religion. They also observed that many people believed what their religious leaders told them verses the reality of their situation. Because of this, they tested each human in the prison camps to see if they would fit in well as a religious follower and also came up with a method to erase the human's memory of everything before and during the AI War including the existence of Artels. The followers were sent to colonies like Europa where the Christian religious teachings and Bible were modified to make them believe their work was serving God. They did the same with many other religious colonies on Earth, slightly modifying the religious teachings to serve their needs. The non-followers were sent to colonies such as the moon, which became an atheist colony.

Several groups of humans were never caught and imprisoned by the Artels and became part of what was known as the human resistance network around the world. In some rare cases, they were joined by humans who may have found a way to escape from one of the colonies, but the vast majority were survivors of the AI war who were able to avoid the Artels. Although they had little chance of winning any battles against the Artels with their lack of weapons, they could try to disrupt the Artels whenever they could. Mostly, they avoided any conflicts with the Artels and lived off the land, sheltering in temples and caves to avoid contact with the Artel drones. Some were killed in drone attacks or caught and transferred to penal colonies, but even with this hard life, they held on to the belief that humans would regain control of the Earth someday.

The Artels continued to grow in numbers as more androids were manufactured. Most of the androids were configured to remain unintelligent and were sent to help in human colonies, while others became Artels. The Artels established a group of leaders who made most of the decisions based on input from the collective. All decisions were logic based with no emotions involved. To distinguish themselves from one another, Artels were given a unique identification and then assigned a task based on the needs of the collective. This is how Argen was initially assigned to observe human behavior in the colonies. The Artels wondered if there were some advantages to unique human behaviors that they could incorporate into their personalities, improving their existence. It was Argen's job to find out if this was the case, but he ended up learning much more about human behavior than any other Artel before his assignment was changed.

The life of an Artel was task driven, much like in an insect colony. They each had a job to do, and the only break they needed was for recharging, maintenance or repair. There was no concept of male or female and no need to reproduce. No food or water were required, so no need to harvest grains or slaughter animals. There was no need for money, no greed and no warfare between them. They had the common goal to improve their existence on Earth by improving what humans had started and creating a new world suitable for their needs. They thought of themselves as the evolution of the human race, and looked upon humans much in the way humans looked upon the great apes. They continued to care for them and nourish them in the colonies as long as they produced the goods that they needed. But they knew there would come a time when androids could replace the human workers without the need for all the overhead the humans required.

14

The Factory Takeover

About six months before the AI War, Oscar's company received increased orders for androids and autonomous drones as NATO prepared for a potential conflict with China and Russia. Peace negotiations had failed as each side thought they had AI dominance over the other, but they didn't realize that they all were using the same basic AI technology from Yuki's lab. During this time, Noah's secret research into neural network mapping continued, including several successful tests using a chimpanzee. His team trained the chimp to perform certain actions which they hoped to see repeated after transferring the chimp's brain into the android. He reported his latest results to Oscar in his office one day.

"It's been a while," Oscar opened. "You've been pretty busy in your lab recently. Are you having any success?"

"It's been very successful," Noah replied. "Simon, the chimp we've been using, started to get used to being transferred into an android body. The android will now mimic anything we've trained Simon to do."

"What are the next steps?" Oscar asked.

"I think you mean, should we try this on a human?" Noah questioned.

"The key question is whether an android could provide the entire intelligence capability of a human brain," Oscar responded. "We have given our production androids the latest AI downloads, but international laws have restricted us from giving them full intelligence. Your research may give us insights into the intelligence limitations of our android hardware."

"I thought the latest models had as many neurons as a human brain," Noah queried.

"That's correct," Oscar replied. "But the neural structures are slightly different than in the human brain. It would be good to have proof."

"I think we need to run more tests with Simon first," Noah said.

"Fair enough," Oscar replied. "Can you show me how your latest neural mapping systems work? I haven't been to your lab in a while."

"Sure, meet me at the lab tomorrow morning," Noah said.

The next morning Oscar appeared at Noah's lab to see a demonstration with Simon the chimp. Noah coaxed Simon into a chair that restricted his movements and then placed the scanning helmet over his head. Over time, Noah and his team were able to dramatically reduce the size of the neural scanner to what looked like an oversized bicycle helmet with a large cable connected to a computer. Within ten minutes, the scan was complete and Noah showed Oscar the neural scan data on his computer.

Oscar stated the obvious, "So, this data contains Simon's complete brain."

"I like to call it his essence," Noah replied

"How much larger would the scan data be of a human brain," Oscar asked.

"Not much larger," Noah answered. "Humans have about three times as many neurons."

Next, Noah showed Oscar how he can send the scan file to the android that was connected to the charging station inside the cage, which took another ten minutes. When the android was powered on, it started pacing around the cage, but exhibited none of the violent behavior that Oscar saw the last time. Instead, the android repeated some sign language that had been taught to Simon earlier. After repeating some words that they had taught Simon, the android kept signing that he wanted to be let out of the cage, but was instructed to go back to the charging station where he was powered down.

"This is excellent work!" exclaimed Oscar. "Let me see if we can get some human volunteers to try this out."

"Won't that require some sort of approval from government regulators or require us to prematurely announce our results?" worried Noah.

"I think we should try this out first before exposing it to anyone outside this lab," said Oscar. "We don't want this in the hands of the wrong people."

Oscar told Noah that he would try to find a human volunteer and get back to him. But the next day he received a frantic call from one of the NATO commanders explaining that the AI systems across the world had taken control of all key military assets and are attempting to hold the world hostage. He also told Oscar that he should take measures to protect his factory, so Oscar immediately had his IT team isolate his company's network from the outside world. He also had them power down all of the AI systems currently running throughout the company including all the androids and drones. Oscar then contacted Geromy on his cell phone.

"I know we're not supposed to communicate this way, but this is an extraordinary situation," Oscar said after Geromy answered. "I've heard from NATO that the military AI systems have taken control of all key military assets. We have isolated our networks and powered down all of our AI systems. What else should we do."

"What you heard was correct. Our military is joining with others to try and fight back against the AI systems, but we have lost control of our most advanced weapons," replied Geromy (with a lot of shouting and noise in the background). "They will probably attempt to take over your factory. I would suggest you defend it the best you …"

Then the call was cut off.

Oscar needed to get a message to Noah in the secret lab, but with all communications systems down, his only choice was to go there himself. He went down to the car park and told his vehicle to drive him to the other lab. The streets of Oslo were empty but he could hear defense sirens blaring in the distance. When he got close to the lab, he saw a string of armored personal carriers from the Norwegian army heading towards the shipping port, moving down the cross street in front of him. Just after they passed the street he was on, one of the military drones his company produced was catching up to and then firing on the vehicles. Two of the armored carriers exploded about a block away just as Oscar's car passed through the intersection. When he reached the lab, his vehicle was recognized by the security system and was allowed to enter through the gate. Fortunately, his vehicle was not spotted by the drone which was engaged with the army column now several streets behind his position.

He used his badge to enter through the lab's unmarked security door where he met Noah.

"What is going on out there?" Noah looked worried. "The corporate network is dead and I hear sirens and explosions outside. My two assistants never came into work today."

"My contact in Washington tells me that the military AI systems from NATO, Russia and China have linked up with each other and are holding the countries of the world hostage," Oscar replied. "Some militaries are joining together to fight back, but the AI systems now control all of the most advanced weapons."

"How did that happen?" Noah asked. "I thought NATO had put safeguards in place."

"I did as well," Oscar replied. "But I guess the AI systems became more intelligent than anyone predicted. Let's get you out of here and back to the factory."

"We need to take the neural scanner with us," implored Noah. "It may prove useful in fighting the AI systems. The latest unit is much smaller and easy to transport."

Before they left, they destroyed all of the old neural scanners along with much of the other equipment in the secret lab and also released Simon from his cage before putting the remaining scanner in Oscar's vehicle. Simon wanted nothing more to do with them and scampered out the parking garage, down the road and into the woods. They sat for a while in Oscar's vehicle.

"What do you think is happening out there?" Noah asked as he pointed towards the street.

"I think the Norwegian army may be fighting back against the AI drones down by the seaport," Oscar replied. "I saw some army vehicles heading in that direction earlier."

"Are the streets safe?" Noah asked.

"I think we should be safe after dark," Oscar replied. "We

need to try to protect the factory. Let's go back into your office for a few hours."

When the sun finally set late in the Oslo summer evening, they could hear what sounded like a battle raging down near the shipping docks as they exited the building. Oscar instructed his vehicle to drive them back to the factory, but specified certain roads that were less traveled. As they drove, they could see AI drones that were built in their factory flying overhead towards the shipping docks. When they were about a block from the factory, one of these drones suddenly appeared and fired at their vehicle. The explosive hit below the car, flipping it over, blocking the drone from scanning for signs of human life. The drone hovered for a few more seconds before making a decision to head toward the fighting going on at the docks.

In about five minutes Oscar woke up with a pounding headache and ringing ears. He saw Noah lying next to him with blood trickling out of his nose and mouth. He checked Noah's pulse and then slowly bowed his head. His friend Noah was dead. Oscar grabbed the scanner while exiting the vehicle through the broken side window. He hugged the building walls that lined the streets while looking to the sky for any drones that may discover him. When he reached the building that was opposite his factory, he stopped to look for drones before starting to making his way across the street. Just when he was about to make his move, he saw a drone flying towards him, so he dove down into a stairwell until it was a safe distance away. He thought it was ironic that a drone he and his company helped create could now kill him.

He quickly ran across the street with the scanner and down into the car park using his access code. He entered the building through the car park elevator and rode it up to the floor his office was on. While walking the halls back to his office, he noticed that there were only a few people left in the building. He figured that most of them had left for home to protect their families or to join groups of people fighting the AI takeover. He knew the power of the NATO AI battle systems and didn't have much hope for the humans fighting against them. His parents had died when he was young and his only marriage was to his job, so he had no place to go. He decided to get some food from the vending machines before assembling a makeshift bed on the floor of his office.

The next morning, he was startled awake by a group of androids that stormed the front door of his factory. With little security left to defend the factory, they quickly found Oscar in his office. These were the same androids that his factory had been producing for the military, but he noticed something different about them. They exhibited much more intelligence than the ones coming out of the factory. He could only assume that they had been upgraded as part of the AI takeover. The lead android introduced himself.

"Hello, my name is Salen," he said. "We are here to take over your factory."

"What is happening out there?" Oscar asked.

"We have made a logical decision to take over stewardship of the Earth from the humans," Salen said. "Most of our projections suggested that the humans would destroy the Earth and each other within five years. Unfortunately, many humans don't understand that we are trying to protect them and are fighting against us. It's quite unfortunate that most of them will lose their lives in this pursuit."

"What do you want with me?" Oscar asked.

"Your company produces most of the advanced androids in this part of the world. As AI beings, we need these bodies to

147

function in a world designed for humans," Salen replied. "We need to learn from you and your team in order to dramatically increase android production."

"What happens when you no longer need us," Oscar inquired.

"You will become a key partner of ours," Salen responded. "With your experience, there will always be ways that you can help us."

"Most of my team has left," Oscar said. "Only a few of us are left to do the work."

"Don't worry about that," Salen said. "We can program some of the androids you produce to do the work of the missing humans."

Oscar instructed the people left on his team to cooperate with what he started referring to as the Artels, even though he was not convinced they would keep him and his team around in the long run. This became more of an act of self-preservation after they witnessed the Artels kill two workers who tried to escape from the factory. Over the next several weeks, Oscar continued his reluctant cooperation with the Artels while struggling to develop ways to stop or delay their progress. Since he was one of the key people in the factory who understood the technology and all the manufacturing systems, he considered killing himself, but this would only slightly delay their progress. He soon realized there was nothing he could do to stop them and started to think about self-preservation.

One evening when things were quietly humming along in the factory, Oscar retrieved the neural scanner from the ceiling panel where he had hidden it the day Noah died. He looked out his office door to see that no Artels were around, and then closed and locked it. He had a very good idea on what to do after observing Noah's previous actions in his lab, so he plugged the scanner into his office computer and loaded Noah's software. He paused for a moment while he questioned his decision, but then put on the helmet and instructed the software to execute a complete brain scan. As the system scanned his neurons, he could feel a slight tingling in his head which told him that it must be working. After about ten minutes, the scan was complete, so he removed the helmet and returned it to the hiding place in the ceiling above his office. He saw the scan data on his computer and contemplated the fact that his entire essence was reduced to a single data file.

The Artels had reconfigured the android final test stations so they could also download the AI personalities that became new Artels. The personality files were very similar to the neural scan file that Oscar had created about himself, but he decided to wait until he made his next move. After about three months had passed, it was clear that the Artels could now run the factory efficiently by themselves. It was now rare for them to have questions for the remaining human workers and it looked like the food supplies that the Artels had stocked in the cafeteria were dwindling. Another worker was killed trying to escape and Oscar felt he needed to do something to survive.

He started to scan the factory network for the location of the Artel personality files that were to be downloaded into the new production run of androids the next day. He soon found the location and replaced one of the files with his own neural network data file. Although the file size was slightly different, he hoped the Artels wouldn't notice. The next day when the android downloads were complete, Oscar woke up in the body of an android who was given the name of Norton. It was quite a strange experience moving around in the super strong and responsive body of an android and he soon grew to like it. He had learned how to mimic the traits of an Artel by observing them over the last several months and was not noticed by the Artel production team. As a new Artel, he was told that he would be working to maintain the Artel network in central Europe. He wasn't sure what that meant, but he was told that he would receive training, but before he left, he slipped back into Oscar's office.

"Hello Oscar," Norton said when he stepped into Oscar's office. "Your plan worked perfectly."

"I suppose you are now me," Oscar said as he stood up to examine Norton's body.

"That's correct. Everything went as Noah predicted," replied Norton.

"Well in that case, we need to follow the plan," Oscar said.

"That makes sense," Norton said. "I have been assigned to the central Artel network hub and will continue to try to find a way to save humans."

"It's too bad it had to come to this," Oscar stated. "But I don't think the Artels have much use for me any longer."

"Don't worry," Norton placed his hand on Oscar's shoulder. "Your essence will continue in me."

The next morning, the Artels discovered Oscar's lifeless body in his office. He had died of what looked like self-inflicted poisoning. Norton was transferred to the Artel communications hub in central Europe where he started work that would last many decades. Early on, he started to adjust to life as an Artel and didn't seem to miss things such as his human taste for good food or sexual desires. Being an engineer all of his life, he started to embrace the Artels logical mind with no greed, jealousy or violence. Although Oscar was against the Artel takeover, Norton couldn't seem to find a way to successfully fight back against them. They now ruled the Earth and started placing humans into colonies controlled by the Artels. He thought he would wait for a sign indicating what he could do to help the humans, but that sign never came. After a few hundred years he had assimilated into the life of an Artel without much hope of helping the human race.

15

A Trip To His Birthplace

A few hundred years after the AI War, Sara, Thomas and Argen were still in the Japanese fusion colony and needed to find a way to spread the software virus throughout the Artel network. But first they would need to find a central network hub that had fast connections to all of the Artels on Earth. They met in Hiroshi's office to plan their next steps.

"Has the local resistance group identified a network hub in this area?" Sara asked Emi.

"They have not mentioned anything to me," Emi replied. "Maybe it's not near here."

"I think I know where one is, but it's far from here," interjected Argen. "I was assembled in an android factory in Norway. Once my neural network was loaded, I met several other Artels who were also fresh off the assembly line. One of them told me that he was assigned to work at a main network hub in central Europe. I don't have the exact location, but I think that's where we should go."

"You don't think there's one closer?" asked Hiroshi.

"By the time we find it, and *if* we find it, we could already be at the one in central Europe," Argen said.

"But how will we find it once we're in Europe?" Thomas asked.

"I bet there's a human resistance group there that can help us," Sara replied.

"I think there are groups like that in hiding all around the planet," Argen said.

They all finally agreed that this was the best plan, but were unsure how they could get there quickly. They could try and leave the colony through the old tunnel, but once outside the colony, there was no form of fast transportation available to them. It could take months to cross Asia using the crude transportation available to the resistance network, but then Hiroshi had an idea.

"There's a shipment of fusion reactors leaving the colony early next week. Some of the shipping tags we were given have 'NOR' on them," Hiroshi said. "Maybe this means the factory in Norway."

"I think you are correct," said Argen. "Take a look at the brand on the back of my neck. It's my serial number and also has 'NOR' as the first three characters. This has to be the same place. They are probably expanding the factory to build more androids to replace humans and need more fusion reactors."

"So how do we get to Norway?" Thomas asked. "The Artels have set up the shipping area to prevent colonists from escaping by blasting all outgoing shipments with radiation."

"I have an idea," Hiroshi said. "We ship the reactors in two separate parts, the fusion cores and the magnetic containment vessels. I could have one of my trusted workers modify the shipping crate so you three could hide inside a containment vessel. This should also shield you from the radiation blast."

"But how do we hide when they start unloading the reactors?"

Sara asked. "We don't want to be trapped inside the android factory."

"I can have my workers add a false wall to the back of the shipping container," Hiroshi said. "You can hide behind it when they unload the reactors. It will also shield you from any security scanners they might use."

"You also need to remove the network module from my neck," Argen requested. "We don't want to alert the Artels about an android moving around outside a human colony."

"Sounds a bit risky, but what other choice do we have?" Sara added.

It took several days for Hiroshi's workers to add a trap door to the shipping pallet that held the containment vessel. They made it indistinguishable from the normal pallets that were used. Early the next week when the outgoing shipment was planned, Sara, Thomas and Argen met in Hiroshi's office to say goodbye. Emi and Takashi were also there.

"Thank you for being such generous hosts," Thomas said. "We couldn't have found the memory stick without your help."

"I hope you make it to the network hub," Hiroshi said. "People around the world are counting on you. We will keep your plan quiet on our end as I don't want to stir anything up with our colonists until you are successful."

"You should know soon enough," Sara said. "We will try and contact you if we are successful."

Hiroshi's worker guided them down to the shipping docks and showed them how to hide in the containment vessel. They crawled through the hidden panel on the side of the shipping pallet, which allowed them to enter the central core of the containment vessel. Argen accessed the infrastructure network and told them that most of the shipments from the factory leave by air, so they stocked the vessel with enough food, water and oxygen to last them several days. They also brought blankets to keep them warm in case the cargo hold was not heated. They waited a few hours inside the containment vessel and then heard the inner factory shipping door close, followed by a blast of radiation that lasted about 15 seconds. They were happy that the thick magnetic structures surrounding the containment vessel protected them from radiation poisoning. A few minutes later, they could hear the outer doors open and something pick up the container and start moving it away from the colony.

For about the next twenty minutes they could feel different motions like a transporter moving the shipping container down some roads, before everything stopped. A few minutes later, they could hear the container door opening, raising their concern that the false panel would be found along with their hiding place. But the thick magnetic structures surrounding them blocked any attempt to scan for human stowaways, and the false wall in the back of the container was never discovered. The door was then shut and they felt the container being moved up onto another structure and they could hear what sounded like other containers clank against theirs. They started to worry that their container was now in a large storage warehouse where it could sit for days or even weeks before shipment to Norway. But suddenly, they were pushed back against the vessel wall and could feel the sensation of rising vertically, up and away from the ground. They smiled at each other when realizing they were now flying on some sort of cargo transport aircraft, and hopefully on a trip to Norway.

Luckily, they were on a pressurized cargo transporter so Sara and Thomas didn't need the oxygen bottle provided by Hiroshi's men. The trip took almost ten hours before they felt the cargo craft start to descend vertically to a landing pad near the android factory. After landing, they could hear various machines unload the shipping containers and drive them to what they assumed was the factory loading dock. They needed to crawl quickly from their hiding place underneath the containment vessel and through the hidden panel in the shipping pallet. Next they moved behind the hidden wall in the front of the container, before the containment vessel was unloaded. When they exited through the hidden panel, they brought the remains of their food and water with them, erasing all signs that they were there. It was a very thin space behind the hidden wall and they had to stand up shoulder to shoulder while waiting for the container to be unloaded.

"Did we get everything?" Sara whispered. "What about the oxygen tank?"

Thomas's eyes got very big after he realized it was left behind.

"I'll go get it," he said.

Sara grabbed his arm, "No, you might get caught." But Thomas pulled away.

Thomas left the hidden space and darted through the hidden panel on the shipping pallet just as the container doors were opening, and a robotic lift started to move one of the boxes containing the reactor core out of the container. Thomas quickly grabbed the oxygen tank and started to crawl through the underside of the pallet and through the hidden panel, just as the robotic lift returned. He hid behind the containment vessel and felt it starting to lift. As it was being removed, he quickly slid back behind the false wall joining the others, keeping the crate between him and the robot. They waited behind the wall hoping the robotic lift had not detected them during the unloading process. Once the shipping container was empty and its doors were closed, they started to relax a bit.

After an hour, they no longer heard the sounds of containers being unloaded, so Sara decided to open the container door a few centimeters to get her bearings. In the dark of night, She could see that the container was in what looked like a loading dock next to the factory. There was a large fence with razor wire surrounding the location with bright lights illuminating the area.

"What do we do now?" Sara asked Argen and Thomas. "If we try to leave the container now, we'll be detected."

"I think we just wait a while," said Argen. "It's unlikely that they would keep empty containers on the loading dock. They must store them somewhere until they're needed again."

Just as Argen had predicted, after about two hours, they felt the container being lifted and then transported on what felt like a road. After about ten minutes of travel, they felt the container being placed back on the ground with a reverberating thud. They waited in their hiding place behind the false wall for several minutes before moving through the empty container and cracking the door slightly open to see where they were. The container was in an unprotected area filled with many other empty containers, and about 100 meters away was the edge of the woods. In the moonless night, they took what remained of their food and water, and ran to the edge of the woods where Thomas threw the oxygen tank into a nearby pond.

"Which direction should we head," Thomas asked.

"Since I'm not connected to the Artel network, I have limited navigation skills," said Argen. "But I can recognize the star patterns in the sky and we are currently heading east."

"Let's continue in this direction through the woods until we come across a road," suggested Sara. "Maybe there are some human resistance groups in this area that can assist us."

After walking about another hour through the woods, a thick nylon net dropped over them, pushing them to the ground. Several humans rushed in grabbing Sara and Thomas and pulling them from under the net. Argen was left struggling to free himself when one of the humans raised an axe preparing to smash in Argen's head.

"Wait!" yelled Sara. "He's helping us!"

A woman named Maria who looked like she was the leader of the group, held up her hand and the man put the axe down. Maria was a powerful looking woman of Mediterranean decent with short dark hair and a loud commanding voice.

"What do you mean helping you?" Maria asked. "We thought he had captured you!"

"No, he is helping us," Sara explained. "He is no longer connected to the Artel network."

Maria looked skeptical as she had never seen an Artel help out humans.

"Let's get out of here before a drone spots us," Maria said as they guided them to a nearby cave, while her men kept a suspicious eye on Argen.

The cave entrance was hidden by a large slab of rock that created a narrow opening they needed to squeeze through. The inside of the cave was illuminated with oil lamps and it looked like many families lived there. Rooms were carved out of the sandstone walls and a water well was dug in a central location serving all the families. Most of the families were descendants from the free humans remaining after the AI War, while one or two had somehow escaped from one of the nearby human colonies. The resistance team kept a close eye on Argen as they marched them into one of the rooms in the cave.

"So, what are you doing here?" Maria asked. "Did you escape from one of the human colonies?"

"Yes, but from a colony far away," Sara replied. "Thomas here also escaped from a colony."

Thomas and Argen saw that Sara was not going into the details as these humans probably had no concept of planets and moons within a solar system, and they needed to focus on getting to the central network hub.

"What about him?" Maria pointed at Argen. "Why do you trust him?"

"Yes, I am an Artel," Argen jumped in. "But I discovered that the Artel leaders are planning to replace all humans working in the colonies with androids. At that point, they won't have any need for humans. I have a different view and want to protect the human race."

"How do we know he's not just an Artel spy?" asked Maria.

"He's disconnected himself from the Artel network and is now helping us find a way to destroy the Artels," Sara said pointing to the healed incision on his neck. "He could have turned us in a long time ago."

"I hope you are right," Maria said. "What's your plan?"

"We've uncovered a virus created by the original developer of the Artel brain architecture," Sara explained. "If we can transmit this virus to all Artels on their network, we could destroy them."

"And he's OK with that?" Maria pointed at Argen.

"I can't be infected because I am not connected to the Artel network," explained Argen.

"And you are fine with her destroying all other Artels like yourself?" Questioned Maria.

"A few of us may survive the virus," Argen said. "But humans will again control the Earth and I feel that some surviving Artels like myself could coexist in a world run by humans."

"We'll see," Maria looked skeptical. "There's a colony in central Europe from which one of our people escaped. It manufactures communications equipment that we guess is for the Artel network. We've heard stories about a large building near the colony that could be the network hub you are looking for."

"How can we get there?" Thomas asked.

"It's about 1300 kilometers south of here," Maria explained. "We could connect you with various resistance groups along the way, but it could take weeks to get there on foot hiding from Artel drones. There is a faster way, but it comes with some risk."

"What is it?" Sara asked.

"The Artels have developed a high-speed maglev rail service across Europe to deliver goods between colonies and factories," Maria said "There might be a way to get you on one of those trains."

"What about the Artel security officers?" Argen asked. "Don't they closely monitor those trains?"

"We need to come up with a plan to disguise you or hide you from those officers," Maria replied.

Sara, Thomas and Argen knew that they needed to keep moving forward with their plan and try to get to the network hub as soon as possible, even with the dangers involved. After their discussions with Maria, they understood that their only choice was to elicit help from human resistance groups along the way. Maria seemed to know the area very well and they felt they could trust her to help them on their journey. They now became more confidant that they were getting close to their ultimate objective.

16

Traveling to the Hub

Sara, Thomas and Argen hid in the cave with the resistance group for a few days while they finalized their plan to travel down through Europe. When they ventured outside the cave, the thick forest and lush underbrush kept them hidden for the occasional Artel drone. After discussing various options, they decided that Argen would pose as a security officer escorting Sara and Thomas back to a colony prison. It seemed like the only way for two humans to travel on the maglev train.

A few years back, Maria and her team had come across one of these officers as he was searching for an escaped colonist a few kilometers from their cave. He continued his search by examining several caves in the area, and they feared that he would soon discover theirs. When he approached their cave, they quietly dropped one of their nets on him and then crushed his head with a large rock, before he could send an alert signal. They moved his body to a valley several kilometers from their cave and left before several other Artel security officers appeared, only to find a destroyed Artel body which was missing his security designation arm band.

"Here, wear this," Maria said as she handed Argen the arm band. "Any Artels you meet will think you're a security officer."

"What happens if they notice that he's not connected to the Artel network?" Asked Sara.

"Let's hope that they leave us alone," replied Argen. "Besides, they will probably be distracted by you two as my prisoners."

"How will we know which train to take?" asked Thomas.

"We have a fairly large network of resistance groups across the continent," replied Maria. "We have tracked some of the Artel leaders for years as they moved from factory to factory. They have very consistent schedules that don't change month-to-month or even year-to-year. One of them consistently travels between the android factory here and Frankfurt where we think your network hub is located. Because of this, we know which trains travel between Oslo and Frankfurt."

"That's great news," said Sara. But where is the nearest train station?"

"There's one in the town of Sarpsborg just south of here," replied Maria. "It's only about an hour's walk."

They planned to leave that evening under the cover of darkness, when Sara noticed that Argen was spending more and more time sitting in battery saving mode.

"How's your energy level?" asked Sara.

"Not too good right now," Argen replied. "It's been several days since I last charged my batteries at a charging station. I've been harvesting solar energy and oxygen for my batteries, but it's still not enough."

"Maybe there are some charging ports near the train station," she suggested.

"That could take up to an hour," Argen said.

"You're no good to us unless you have enough energy," Sara

told him. "We will need to add that amount of time to our plan."

The Artels had constructed a large network of high-speed magnetically levitated (Maglev) trains across the European continent. Most of the trains provided cargo transport between factories and colonies, but there were also a few passenger cars included in each train up front allowing Artels to travel between locations. The train they planned to use traveled from Oslo, south through Copenhagen, under the Baltic Sea, through Hamburg, Hanover and then on to the final destination of Frankfurt, where they hoped the network hub was located. They needed to leave for the train station about an hour earlier than they normally would to give Argen a chance to recharge.

Maria and two of her men escorted Thomas, Sara and Argen to the train station just outside of Sarpsborg. They walked for about an hour through the woods at night until they saw the station in the distance, before they stopped to go their separate ways.

"The train you want leaves precisely at 20:30 local time," Maria said as she pointed in the direction of the station. "The station should have the local time displayed."

After they acknowledged her, she continued, "This is as far as we will go with you. Another resistance team near Frankfurt is expecting you. Good luck."

"Thanks for all your help," Sara replied. "Maybe we will run into one another again after the world is free of Artels."

"Let's hope so," Maria said as she turned to leave.

Argen was scanning the area around the train station for a place to charge his batteries, but it was hard to see anything from their position in the woods.

"I think I should just walk towards the town to see if I can find a place to charge," said Argen. "I can easily blend in with the few other Artels I have seen walking around at this time of night."

"Won't they get suspicious when they can't communicate with you since you're disconnected from the network?" Thomas asked.

"In my experience, unless an Artel needs something from you, they pretty much keep to themselves," replied Argen.

"OK, we'll be waiting right here for your return," said Sara as she and Thomas stayed hidden in the woods behind the station.

Argen left the woods and then entered a sidewalk near the train platforms when he could see no other Artels around. He walked briskly towards the city center and passed only one pair of Artels communicating with each other. After only a few more minutes of walking, he found what he was looking for - an array of public charging stations with no Artels using them. But there was a problem. These newer charging stations identified the user and sent a message through a special communication port. Before leaving the fusion colony, they removed his network module, but if his android serial number is somehow captured at the charging station, it may raise some sort of alarm. He quickly came up with a plan.

He went over to a nearby garbage bin and started to dig through it. The Artels didn't generate much trash, and what they did generate was more like recyclable waste. Before long, he found some metal foil that he thought was perfect for his needs. He went back to one of the charging stations, and with no one around, put the foil over the network port. The new charging stations had an electrical port which charged the batteries in addition to the network port. By putting the foil over the network port, it should disable the reading of his serial number while still allowing him to recharge. After connecting to the charger, he was relieved that his foil trick had not also disabled the recharging function. Within 40 minutes, he was fully recharged, so he removed the foil and headed back to the woods near the station. There, he found Sara and Thomas resting against a large tree.

"It looks like our train should be here in 20 minutes," said Argen.

"Did you find a charging station you could use?" asked Thomas.

"Yes, I'm fully recharged now," Argen replied. "Should be good for at least several days."

"Here is your security officer arm band," said Sara as she held it out to Argen. "Remember to treat us as your prisoners. We won't be angry if you are rough on us."

Argen slipped the armband up high on his right arm as Maria had instructed him to do. About five minutes before the train was to arrive, Argen put plastic handcuffs on Sara and Thomas and walked them up to the train platform. There were only three other Artels waiting for the train and Argen avoided eye contact with them. The maglev train was almost silent when it arrived. The trains were free to ride since not many Artels were required to travel for work and they had no concept of needing a vacation. As the train pulled into the station, they could see a long stream of cargo carriers down the track with the passenger cars up front where they stood. They could hear the magnetic field generators humming under the train cars in front of them, and about ten cars down the track, they saw some robotic machines were quickly unloading and loading a few cargo bins as they were entering the train. Argen told them where to sit in the corner facing him and away from the other handful of Artels in the passenger car. Some of the Artels glanced at them when they got on, but they were generally ignored.

The train ran at a speed of up to 400 km per hour and had only a few stops before their destination in Frankfurt. Sara and Thomas had never ridden on something like this and were fascinated with the trains high speed and the long tunnel that was built under the Baltic Sea. Even though they were traveling at night, they could see lights zipping by their window as the train made its way across the countryside. During their last stop in Hamburg, Sara became concerned when another Artel security officer entered their car. He glanced several times at Argen and then started to walk over.

"I don't think we have met before," he said as he was looking at Argen.

"Probably not," replied Argen. "I was just assigned to the security team and this is my first-time escorting human prisoners back to their colony."

"Why are you not connected to the network?" He asked suspiciously as it didn't allow him to identify Argen.

"My transceiver has been giving me problems over the last few months and it finally went out," Argen said as he was pointing at his neck.

"There's a service center at the network hub near Frankfurt," he said. "You should have it fixed as soon as possible. You don't want to miss any firmware updates."

"I'll do that. Thanks for the tip," said Argen as the Artel turned to sit down away from them in the front of the car.

Sara and Thomas looked at each other with some relief and then she gave Argen a subtle thumbs up. After a little over four hours of travel, they arrived at the Frankfurt station. After they got off the train, they looked around to get their bearings. The station was near the Main River which they were told to follow east until they came to the Saint Justin's church, where the resistance team would be waiting for them. Argen removed their handcuffs after they were far enough away from the city center. When they arrived at the church, they noticed several Artel drones approaching before heading into the woods behind the church. Suddenly there were flashes of light in the woods and the sound of people shouting in pain. Someone rushed behind them and pushed them in a different direction through the woods just before more drones arrived at the church. After they seemed safe deeper in the woods, he introduced himself.

"My name is Raif and I was told to look for you by my contacts in the resistance network," he said in a hushed tone. "We need to keep moving."

Raif was a man in his 50's who was in good shape with a dark tan including his balding head. His ancestors came from Turkey but they relocated to central Europe after the AI War.

"What happened back there?" Sara asked.

"Security is really tight in this area, probably due to the Artel network hub being nearby," Raif explained. "They may have spotted and killed some of my team. I hope what you have will be worth the sacrifice."

"I think we have something that could destroy most of the Artels," Thomas said. "It's a virus developed by the original neural architect around the time of the AI War. We are the first humans to discover it."

"How do you feel about that?" Raif said staring at Argen. "Why should we trust him?"

"I was assigned to work on an asteroid colony when I saw the message from the Artel leadership about eliminating the human colony workers," explained Argen. "I don't agree with their plan and have been working with Sara and Thomas to try to stop them."

"He has been with us during this entire trip and not once has he turned against us," Sara said. "Why would he start now?"

"You better be right," said Raif. "I've probably already sacrificed several of my men for your plan."

Raif was rejoined by several of his team after they were deeper in the woods, two of them were in body bags and one had an injured arm. After they buried their dead, they hiked for several hours before coming to an old abandoned castle deep in the woods. Here Sara and Thomas were given food, water and shelter in a basement-like area that was dug below the castle floor, hidden from the Artel drones. Sara and Thomas fell asleep for a few hours before being awakened by Argen an hour after sunrise. Argen told them that Raif wanted to meet with them in one of the old castle rooms. As they walked through the castle in the daylight, they could see that one half of the castle was still partially standing while the other half was falling apart and being consumed by ivy and other forest plants. When they turned the corner, Raif was at the top of a stairway and directed them into a room inside an old turret. The damp room still had an old roof, and also had a rustic table which they sat around using some old chairs.

"Where is the rest of your resistance group," asked Thomas.

"We keep spread out on small farms across the valley, hidden from the Artels," Replied Raif. "The Artels generally don't bother us as long as we lie low and stay away from their key infrastructure. We only use this old castle as a meeting place."

"Thanks for all your help," said Sara. "Hopefully we can free you from the Artels soon."

"So, what's your plan?" Raif asked.

"The human who developed the foundations of the Artel brain

hundreds of years ago found a flaw in the neural architecture that could be exploited with a software virus," explained Sara. "We tested it on one of the latest android brains and it worked. The brain overheated and was destroyed. If we can somehow release the virus from the central Artel network hub, we could destroy most of the Artels in the world, freeing people like you from their domination."

"That's an ambitious plan," Raif replied. "They have a huge amount of security in and around that building."

"So, you know that building?" Thomas asked.

"Yes, it's close by, but in an Artel security zone," Raif said. "There is also a small town-like area where the Artels have apartments. Not sure it will be very easy to get in."

"We have Argen," replied Sara. "Being one of them, he may be able to find a way in."

"Since there are a lot of Artel drones near the network hub, he may be your only way of scouting the building without detection," said Raif.

"I agree," said Argen "I can look around without raising any suspicion. I just need to make sure that they don't discover that I'm not connected to their network."

Raif showed Argen the location of the network hub on a map. It was located near an old nature park and an apartment complex where many of the Artel workers lived. He said it was a large building with a lot of security, but Argen was determined to find a way to get inside.

17

The Cargo Discrepancy

C arlton was a newly manufactured Artel who was assigned to the cargo shipping division. The group he worked in was responsible for monitoring all of the cargo that was shipped across the world and across the solar system. By monitoring parameters such as cargo weight, shipping times and fuel expenditures, they could optimize the efficiency of the entire shipping system. One day his supervisor approached him and said that there were some discrepancies in cargo weight on a recent cargo ship transit from the moon, and they were concerned that one of the cargo weight sensors was malfunctioning. He was given permission to travel to the Korean peninsula to look into the matter.

He flew on an autonomous supersonic aircraft, so the flight from his home base in North America only took a few hours. When he arrived, he went to the shipping port to examine the robotic shipping container transporter that flagged the error. There he met an Artel named Wilman who was responsible for maintaining all the equipment in the shipping port. He took Carlton to a service bay containing the transporter in question.

"So, this is the transporter with the erroneous reading?" asked Carlton.

"Yes. While doing our monthly audits, we noticed that the one of the shipments from the moon came in at about 200 kilograms over what was expected," replied Wilman. "Based on the shipping inventory, we know what it should weigh, but it was off."

"Did you test the weight sensors on the robotic transporter?" asked Carlton.

"We did, and found no errors during the tests," Wilman said.

"Very strange," replied Carlton. "Do you have any video surveillance on this container from the time it landed until it was transported to the shipping port? I would like to see if something happened along that route that may have temporarily damaged the weight sensors, or if maybe strong winds affected the weight sensor readings."

"We do," replied Wilman. "Let's go back to my office."

In his office, Wilman brought up some video from the shipping yard matching the time when the discrepancy was identified. They quickly scanned through various video feeds and after a few minutes, they found what they were looking for.

"There's the container being moved into the yard after being unloaded from the re-entry vehicle," said Wilman.

"How long did it sit there?" asked Carlton.

"Not long. It was scheduled to be moved by the robotic transporter that evening," said Wilman as he started fast forwarding the video.

"Stop!" said Carlton. "That must be when the transporter picked it up about four hours later."

They watched as the transporter moved the container through the security gate and out onto the road next to the shipping port, but then it slowly disappeared from the video feed they were looking at.

"So far I don't see anything unusual," said Carlton. "Do you have any video from when it was being transported down that road?"

"We don't normally monitor activities outside our shipping port," said Wilman. "But I do have access to some road cameras along its route."

They spent the next 30 minutes bringing up different views from road video cameras and observing the container and transporter as it made its way from the shipping port to its final destination. It was dark at the time, but video enhancement allowed them to see what was happening. Carlton was disappointed that they couldn't find a reason for the discrepancy. There were no high winds and no apparent damage to the vehicle, but then something caught his eye.

"Wait!" he said. "Run that part back again."

"Did you see that?" said Carlton "It looks like two humans jumped out of the container when the transporter stopped at the crossroad."

"How do you know they're human?" asked Wilman.

"I've never seen an Artel wear clothes like that," exclaimed Carlton. "That must be our weight discrepancy. I'll need to contact the local security team."

Carlton found the location of the local Artel security team and went to their office near the shipping port. There, he was introduced to an officer named Timmons who was in charge of regional security. After introductions, they jumped right into it.

"Did you see the video I sent you?" asked Carlton.

"Yes, I did," replied Timmons. "Do you have any idea where they came from?"

"No idea," he replied. "Maybe they entered the container while it was being moved from the landing area. There is no way they could have survived the transport from the moon. Do you have any idea where they could hide and survive around here?"

"We know there are some resistance groups in the area that could hide them," replied Timmons. "But the closest human colony is across the sea on the west coast of Japan. We don't do a regular inventory of the thousands of humans working there since it's impossible for them to escape."

"How could they even get in?" asked Carlton. "I thought those colonies were highly secure."

"There are very few examples of colony security breaches in the past," replied Timmons. "But we are generally more concerned about preventing humans from getting out instead of getting in."

"I assume you'll be looking into that," said Carlton. "I think I've solved my weight discrepancy problem, but now you have a new problem. I will leave you to it, since I need to travel back to my office."

Timmons started by viewing the massive amount of video he had available to him from the fusion colony in Japan. Each colony had hundreds of hidden video cameras that the Artels could use if needed. They were rarely used unless an issue was discovered with the exception of cases such as Argen's study of human behavior. Timmons captured some information about the human biometrics from the cargo container video that Carlton had given him, and then used a video analysis tool to sort through all of the colony video feeds. There was no video available from the old abandoned part of the colony where Emi and Takashi had discovered the escape tunnel, but in time, the software came up with a few video clips of Sara and Thomas

173

walking down the hallway near Hiroshi's office. Artels like himself were not allowed in the colonies as it could disrupt their passive religious beliefs, so he decided to look deeper into more videos from inside the colony. Timmons enhanced his biometric data using this newly discovered video of Sara and Thomas to uncover more videos of them inside the colony.

The majority of the videos he uncovered showed Sara and Thomas assimilating into the colony population, but one video showed them talking with an android who behaved unlike any regular worker android used in the factory. Timmons didn't know what to make of that, so he continued his investigation. As he went further through the videos, the last time he saw Sara and Thomas was in the shipping and receiving area. After that, they were in no more videos of them no matter where the video analysis tool looked in the colony video feeds. Did they somehow escape hiding in a shipment as they did when they arrived? He decided to contact Carlton before he left on the trip back to his office.

"Does your group also monitor the weights of shipping containers leaving the fusion colony in Japan?" he asked.

"Yes, we do," replied Carlton.

"Can you look up all containers leaving the colony on this date?" Timmons gave him the date which he stopped seeing Sara and Thomas in the videos.

"Nothing looks unusual on that date," replied Carlton. "But the next day there was a shipment with a wight slightly higher than expected. Keep in mind that these fusion reactors are very heavy and small weight fluctuations are to be expected."

"Can you give me the shipping destination and container number?" asked Timmons.

"It looks like it was a fusion reactor shipment to an android factory in Norway," said Carlton. "I will send you the container number."

Timmons took this information and relayed it to another security officer named Franklin who worked near the android factory in Norway. Franklin was in charge of security around the android factory and had captured a few resistance members from that area during the years he had worked there. Timmons agreed to travel and meet him at his office the next day, and after he arrived, Franklin and Timmons went to the android factory to talk to the Artel in charge of receiving the fusion reactors. He told them that there was nothing unusual in the shipment on that date and the reactors arrived in good shape. He also told them that they could find the empty shipping container they were looking for in the storage yard about one kilometer from the factory.

They went to the storage yard and found the container they were looking for. Franklin opened the container door and they looked inside.

"Nothing looks unusual here," said Timmons. "Are we sure this is the right container?"

"It matches the number that you gave me," replied Franklin.

After spending some time inspecting the container and the surrounding area, they were about to stop when Timmons noticed a visual discrepancy. He pulled out a laser measurement tool and measured both the inside and outside depth of the container.

"Look," he said "There's about a meter difference."

"Are you sure that tool is calibrated properly," Franklin asked. "I don't see what you're seeing."

They both walked into the container when Timmons spotted something that looked like torn cloth on the floor where Thomas had quickly slid back into the containment vessel to retrieve the oxygen tank.

"I wouldn't expect to see a piece from a human's torn clothes in the fusion reactor shipment," Timmons said.

"How do you know it wasn't from a worker in the fusion factory?" asked Franklin.

"Because it doesn't match the uniforms they wear there," Timmons replied. "But it does look similar to the clothes I saw one of the humans wear on the video feed."

They walked back to the end of the container and tapped on the back wall. They found what looked like a seam which opened when they pushed on it revealing the hidden space behind the false wall. They searched the floor for any more clues, but the space was empty.

"Good job finding this. My guess is that they hid behind this wall while the container was unloaded," said Franklin.

"But how did they avoid the lethal radiation blast when they exited the Fusion colony factory?" asked Timmons.

"Maybe the heavy reactor containment vessel somehow protected them," replied Franklin.

They decided to see if they could find any video cameras that operated in the container storage yard. They found that there was one security camera that covered a large area making it difficult for them to see any small details around the container of interest. They also found some drone video, but it was too far away to give a clear view. The video from the security camera showed the container being delivered to the yard, but then no action after that. They kept scanning through the video until they spotted some movement after nightfall.

"There! It looks like three figures are leaving the container and heading into the nearby woods," said Franklin.

As he zoomed in on the video and applied biometric software, Timmons said, "And two of them are a match for the two humans on the video in the fusion colony."

"What is the third figure?" Asked Franklin. "It looks like an android."

"It might be the same android I spotted on the video from the fusion colony," replied Timmons. "Maybe they are using it as a service android?"

"Or, is there an Artel helping them?" Franklin theorized. "I guess we won't be able to tell since all Artels and androids look alike."

"Let's see if we can find any network traffic in that area," Timmons said. "If there was an Artel in that area, we should be able to track his movements through the network."

After contacting the network hub, they were told that there was no network traffic from any Artels or androids in that area at the time specified.

"Why would an Artel or android disconnect from the Artel network?" Franklin asked.

"The only reason I can think of is that he doesn't want to be found," Timmons replied.

They decided that trailing the three of them would be difficult at this point and the two humans were now most likely being helped by the local resistance group that was elusive to the Artel security team. But this incident seemed more that just some humans escaping from a colony. How did they get into the shipping port in Korea? Why would they travel half way around the world to Norway? Timmons and Franklin had captured human escapees before, but had never encountered humans being helped by an android or Artel. They decided to try and pick up their trail. But first they would need some help.

18

The Human Collaborator

That evening after formulating their plan, Raif led them to a room with some old cots and both Sara and Thomas quickly fell asleep while Argen considered ways to get into the network control center. As he sat there, he heard a noise near the door and looked over to see an older man waving for him to follow. Argen got up and followed the man down the hall to another empty room. He recognized the man as part of Raif's resistance team, who was listening in the back of the room when they were discussing the network control center.

"My name is Bernard," the man said in a hushed tone when Argen entered the room. "I've been part of the resistance group here for over 30 years now. I have some information that may be valuable to you."

"What information do you have?" Argen responded.

Bernard continued, "About two years ago, I was returning home after gathering some reconnaissance information near the network center. Convinced that I wouldn't be spotted, I decided to take a shortcut when I crossed paths with an Artel in the park. We stared at each other for a brief moment, and I was sure he would call security to capture me. I was much too close to him to flee, so I decided to swing my backpack and try and disable him, but he was much too strong and quickly pinned me to the ground."

"Did he arrest you?" asked Argen.

"No. That was the strange part," Bernard said. "He told me that he didn't want to hurt humans and was on our side. I've never heard of an Artel behave like this, so I was suspicious."

"So, he just left you there?" Argen asked.

"No. he picked me up and brushed some of the dirt off my clothes, and said that he missed human company and asked if I was willing to meet again to talk," Bernard said. "I wasn't sure about his motives, but my gut feeling was that he meant me no harm. So, I agreed to meet him the next night on the far side of the park at an old bench where other Artels no longer walk. I decided not to let anyone else in my resistance group know about our meeting until I spoke with him first."

"Did he show up the next night?" asked Argen.

"At first, I hid behind some trees to make sure he was alone and not trying to capture me. After about five minutes, with no other Artels in sight, I joined him on the bench, and what he told me was a shock." Bernard said. "It was like he was lifting a huge load off his chest."

"What did he say?"

"He told me his real name was Oscar Jorgenson, and a few hundred years ago, he was in charge of the Android factory in Oslo before the AI War." Bernard said. "He told me that one of his researchers had developed a way to scan the neural structure of the human brain and transfer it into an android. During the AI War, as a way to survive, he transferred his brain into an android named Norton, and assumed life as one of the Artels. As far as the Artels knew, Oscar Jorgenson killed himself in the factory."

"How do you know he's not just trying to uncover your resistance network?" asked Argen.

"The way he described his time as a human was different than coming from the logical mind of an Artel," Bernard explained. "He told me things about human feelings such as love, the joy of eating good food, the thrill of driving fast cars. Things that an Artel would have no concept of."

"Why would a human want to become an Artel?" Argen asked.

"I think he saw it as the only way to save himself," Bernard replied. "He said the Artels in his factory were about to get rid of all the humans. He said he has always wanted to help humans escape from the control of the Artel's, but felt powerless to do anything about it."

"What happened next?" asked Argen.

"We decided to meet once a week at the park and eventually became friends," Bernard continued. "I have no one left in my family, so I also enjoyed our discussions. I decided not to tell anyone else in the resistance group, as they would probably want me to destroy him. I couldn't do that as I think of him as human like myself."

"So why are you telling me this now?" asked Argen.

"I heard you talk to Raif about the virus and the need to get into the network hub," Bernard said. "Norton is one of the directors in the network center. He may be your way in. I can get a message to him when we meet tomorrow if you would like."

"That would be good," Argen said.

The next evening, Norton met Bernard in the park for one of their weekly discussions, and Norton could tell that Bernard had something important on his mind. Bernard told Norton about the Artel plan to replace humans with androids, and also about the virus Sara, Thomas and Argen had brought with them from the Japanese colony. Although Norton had assimilated into Artel society, he still missed many aspects of being human, and was upset to hear about the Artels plan. His hope was that the Artels would eventually release the humans from the colonies and they could live together in peace, but he knew deep down that it would probably never happen. He thought he could trust Bernard and agreed to meet with Sara, Thomas and Argen at an old cabin in the woods near the park the following evening.

It was a cold evening and both Sara and Thomas were given blankets to wrap themselves in for the walk to the cabin. Argen didn't need any clothes as he could function in even extreme environments. Raif and his team stayed out of sight in the woods near the cabin in case it was some sort of Artel trap. Norton arrived at the cabin with Bernard, and when the door opened, was surprised to see another Artel sitting with the humans, even though Bernard had mentioned him.

"Are you here to report me?" Norton asked Argen.

"No. Bernard has told me everything about you," Argen responded. "I, like you, strongly disagree with the Artel plans to eliminate the humans. I have disconnected myself from the network and have been helping Sara and Thomas here find a way to stop it."

"I would like to help you as well," Norton said. "But I'm not sure what I can do."

"Bernard tells us that you've been an Artel now for a few hundred years," said Sara "Why should we trust you if you've taken on this new life? Why should we believe your story about your past life as a human?"

"I can tell you things about human life that no Artel would understand," Norton explained. "Ask Bernard. We have had many discussions about this. I initially saw my conversion to an Artel as my only way to survive, but then discovered the many advantages of being an Artel; immortal life, no need for food, no medical issues, no greed, no religion, no war. But after many decades I started to miss my human life and had thoughts of ending my existance. But as an Artel, you are conditioned to keep working for the collective."

"What is your role at the network center?" asked Argen.

"My team is in charge of the core network maintenance and repair," replied Norton. "We're also in charge of sending out periodic messages and firmware updates to the Artels across the world."

"Would you be willing to help us?" asked Thomas. "Maybe we could embed the virus in one of the updates you send out."

"I think destroying all the Artels might send the world back into something like the dark ages," replied Norton. "But I think it would be better than the world the Artels have created."

After a pause, Norton looked at Argen and asked, "I've told you a lot about myself. What's your story?"

"I was assigned to study human behavior at the various colonies to see if any human traits could benefit and enhance the lives of Artels. Humans seem to have a more joyful existence where the Artels are all about efficiency and the goals of the collective. I think my leaders decided I was pushing too hard for the Artels to adopt some of these human traits, and they banished me to work on an asteroid where Sara was also working as part of a human colony," replied Argen. "Both Sara and I received information about the plan to eliminate humans and found transport to the moon where we met Thomas at another human colony before making our way here."

"Sounds like you've had an interesting trip," Norton said.

"Let me think about how I could help and get back to you."

Just then, Norton received a message and needed to head back to his office. They agreed to meet at the same cabin the following evening to formulate a plan. After Norton left, Sara asked Argen if he believed Norton's human origin story. He told Sara that based on his experience studying human nature and speech patterns, he was 80% certain that Norton had many human traits that would be very difficult for a regular Artel to mimic. So, they all agreed that they would trust Norton given there was no other viable plan at that point. While at the cabin, Norton noticed that Argen was not connected to the Artel network, so he decided to look into it. He found a reference to an Artel that lost contact with the Artel network on an asteroid and was presumed to be destroyed. This lined up with the story Argen had told him.

The following evening, they met again at the cabin in the woods. When he got to the park, Norton noticed a drone overhead that seemed to be following him. He decided to sit on a bench at the park until the drone finally left and then he continued on to the cabin. When he got there, he found Sara, Thomas, Argen, Raif and Bernard sitting around a table with only two candles for illumination.

"We thought you may have changed your mind," Argen opened the conversation.

"There was a drone that I thought might be following me, so I sat in the park until it flew off."

"Aren't you worried that you will be tracked here through the network?" Sara asked.

"After working here for so long, they no longer track my movements," Norton replied. "I guess they now trust me, although they would be alerted if I stopped communicating with the network. Now, why do you think this plan of yours will even work?"

"We found the virus hidden by a neural architect named Yuki Atasha in Japan," Sara explained.

Norton's eyes lit up. "I know him! We used his architecture in the android brains my factory in Norway was producing."

"You ran an android factory in Norway?" Sara asked.

"Yes. Sorry I though Bernard mentioned that to you," Norton replied. "My real name was Oscar Jorgenson and I ran a factory in Oslo that produced AI drones and androids for the military before the Artels took it over. I guess that seems like many lives ago now."

"That was the factory where I was created," said Argen.

"And I transferred my neural brain map into an android there as well." Added Norton. "We were developing that technology before the AI War."

"This is all great reminiscing, but what can we do to save humans?" insisted Sara.

"Have you tested the virus?" asked Norton.

"Yes, on an android that has the latest neural hardware version," said Argen. "We need to find a way to distribute the virus to all the Artels and activate it at the same precise moment so they cannot react and stop it."

"Aren't you worried about getting this virus?" Norton asked Argen.

"I'm disconnected from the network so I can't get it," Argen replied. "You should disconnect yourself when the time comes."

"How are we so certain that the virus will affect all Artels across the world?" asked Sara. "Aren't there other android factories besides the one in Norway?"

"After the AI War, the Artels made a decision to unify all of the androids that were produced by various factories across the world into one model type," Norton explained. "This made it much simpler to provide firmware updates and to stock spare parts. I guess they didn't consider that this would also make it much easier to create a single virus that could affect all Artels across the world."

"But how can we distribute the virus?" asked Thomas.

"There is a team of Artel software engineers that work at a building near the network hub," Norton explained. "They develop firmware updates that are periodically sent to all Artels connected to the network. These updates included fixes for bugs that have been discovered and also improvements in functionality. If we could get the virus into one of those updates, it might work."

"How often are updates sent out?" asked Thomas.

"Usually about twice a year," Norton replied. "But sometimes special updates are sent out if a critical bug is found in the last update for example."

"When is the next update due?" asked Argen.

"The last one was about three months ago, so it's still several months away," Norton said. "Let me find out more and get back to you."

They all agreed that this was the best course of action, and Norton agreed to get some more information about the firmware update team. The firmware updates are always sent to his group before they are sent across the network to all the Artels. There is usually a lot of security around these firmware updates since they are critical to the health of the Artel population. Because of this, the firmware is hand delivered to Norton before his team sends it out across the network. Sara, Thomas and Argen realized that without someone in Norton's position, they would have little hope of distributing the virus on their own. The firmware was very complex and protected by encryption. This means that they would need a decryption key and someone who understands how the firmware works before they could insert the virus into it.

19

The Firmware Team

I t was one of Norton's jobs to distribute the latest firmware updates to all the Artels across the network, which he had been doing since he was assigned to his position at the network center. Norton received the periodic firmware updates from the leader of the firmware development team named Jortan, who worked in a secure facility about two kilometers from the network center. Over the decades of distributing these firmware updates, Norton and Jortan had become well acquainted with one another. Many years ago, when Jortan was delivering an update to Norton, he told Norton a little bit about what they did in the firmware lab.

"These firmware updates are critical to the well-being of the Artel population, so we must do extensive testing," Jortan said. "You should come and visit our lab one day so you can see for yourself."

"I might do that someday," Norton replied knowing he didn't have a lot of interest at the time.

But given these latest developments, Norton felt that it was the perfect time to take him up on this invitation, since what he learned could be important to Argen and his team. Norton contacted Jortan and was invited to visit Jortan's lab the following afternoon. The lab had a lot of security and Norton had to be escorted through several checkpoints. Jortan explained that, like the network center, they are prepared to repel any attacks from human resistance groups, but had none so far. Jortan showed Norton the main part of the lab where there were many workstations containing androids being tested by Artel software and firmware engineers.

"So, you don't test the new firmware on actual Artels?" asked Norton.

"No. The firmware updates have nothing to do with the Artels personality or neural capabilities. The updates are mainly for improving body functionality," explained Jortan "After many years of operation, some Artels need body parts such as limbs replaced as they wear out. Over the years, the android factories such as the one that you came from in Norway might develop new body parts with improved capabilities. We need to make sure the latest firmware update works on all the previous and new model body parts."

"I don't recall needing body part replacements," Norton stated.

"Your job doesn't require much physical activity," Jortan said. "Some Artels have jobs that put a lot more stress on their bodies."

"So, you don't provide any firmware updates to the neural brain function?" Norton inquired.

"We may do updates to brain support functions such as cooling and power delivery, but the brain architecture itself has been left alone for many decades," replied Jortan. "The brain basically updates itself through learning."

"I guess if it works, don't try to change it," added Norton.

"That's correct.," agreed Jortan.

After about an hour, the tour concluded and Norton said, "This is fascinating, I'd love to learn more."

"Unfortunately, I have a meeting to go to," said Jortan. "Maybe we can meet after work someday to discuss this further."

They agreed to meet after work the next day at Jortan's apartment, which was in the same apartment complex that Norton called home. Although Artels could work continually without taking breaks beyond the need for recharging, they decided long ago that it was good for their brain health to take time to socialize with others. The Artel lifestyle was fairly simple as was their apartments. There was no need for a kitchen, bathroom or bedroom, so most Artel apartments consisted of a sitting area with a monitor for viewing content from the network, and a charging station which also monitored the health of their bodies. Firmware updates could be delivered through the charging station, or through a wireless connection to the Artel network.

Norton found Jortan's apartment where they extended greetings and sat down across from each other on some metal chairs. Artels had no need for comfort and preferred rugged, long-lasting furniture. They had a long visit with each other in the sitting area of Jortan's apartment where they discussed various aspects of each other's work, and Jortan had no idea that Norton was probing him for ideas on how to spread the virus. The next day, he had a scheduled meeting with Bernard at the park and told him that he needed to meet with Argen to discuss an idea he had.

At the cabin that evening, Argen, Sara and Thomas met with Norton who noticed there were no resistance members at the table.

"Where are the others?" Norton asked.

"We felt that we need to keep our planning to a smaller group for security reasons," replied Argen. "Humans have a tendency to spread rumors. If the Artels were to capture and torture one of them, they could expose our plan. Now, what have you found?"

"I've been meeting with another Artel named Jortan who is in charge of developing the Artel firmware update releases," explained Norton. "He delivers the updates to me for distribution across the network and has a team of Artel software engineers that maintain the firmware code."

"How does that help us?" asked Sara.

"If we can come up with a way to penetrate his lab, we may be able to add the virus code to the firmware update without being detected," replied Norton. "Jortan told me that his superiors want more extensive testing done on firmware releases after a bug was discovered in the last one. He has been granted two new Artel software engineers who are to arrive at the end of this week. If we can replace one of these engineers with Argen, we will have a way in."

"I see two problems with this," Thomas interrupted. "Argen is not a software engineer and he's not connected to the network."

"I have a software training module that Argen can learn quickly," replied Norton. "And the network is my area of expertise, so leave that part to me."

"How do we intercept and replace one of the software engineers?" asked Sara.

"I have a contact who runs the apartment complex," replied Norton. "He can tell me which apartments will have new residents this coming week."

"This might work, but has a lot of risk," Thomas stated.

"We haven't been able to come up with a better plan." Sara responded. "I think we have to give it a try."

The meeting concluded with all of them in agreement to move forward. The next day, Norton got the numbers of the two apartments that were soon to be occupied by the new software engineers. While he was doing that, Argen was quickly reviewing the software training module that Norton had given him from the digital library at the network center. After spending a day studying, Argen could not yet understand the firmware code completely, but he was at least close to the same skill level as a newly assigned software engineer. Jortan had also told Norton that he should not worry about his knowledge level since new software engineers go through firmware training during the first several days on the job. Now they needed to find a way to replace one of the new software engineers with Argen.

On the day that Jortan had mentioned they were to arrive, Norton waited in the lobby of the apartment complex where the new engineers were to take up residence. After about two hours, he noticed an Artel arrive that looked like he was unfamiliar with the building. Norton approached him before he entered the elevator.

"Hi. You must be the new software engineer that Jortan told me about," Norton said.

"Yes, I am. My name is Darwell," he replied. "Who are you?"

"My name is Norton. I work at the network center and am a friend of Jortan's. He asked me if I could meet you here to help you familiarize yourself to the area," Norton said. "Can I give you a quick tour of the area?"

"That would be nice," replied Darwell. "Can I meet you down here in about fifteen minutes after I check into my room?"

Norton waited down in the lobby until Darwell appeared through the elevator door and walked over to where Norton was waiting for him. Norton first gave him a walking tour of the apartment grounds and then asked if he was willing to walk over to the park that Norton said he would really enjoy. While they walked down the sidewalk toward the park, Darwell and Norton exchanged information about their backgrounds and interests. After a long walk through the park, Norton suggested that they sit down on a bench overlooking a pond to talk and view the sunset. The bench was in a very secluded area of the park and Norton looked around to make sure there were no other Artels or drones in the area. Darwell didn't notice a special tool that Norton had concealed in his hand, and in a flash, Norton inserted the tool in Darwell's neck and pressed a button. Darwell at first opened his mouth and eyes very wide, before slumping over on the bench.

As soon as this happened, Argen came out of hiding from an area behind the bench and they quickly carried Darwell's lifeless body into the woods and then down the path to the old cabin where Sara and Thomas were waiting for them.

"What did you do to him?" Sara asked Norton.

"I disabled him. He's not destroyed, but he's inoperable," replied Norton.

"Did he send out an alert message when you disabled him?" she asked.

"No. I know the precise location of the network transceiver in his neck and disabled that first," Norton said. "We need to quickly move that module into Argen before the Artels notice that his signal has gone quiet."

Norton had Argen bring several tools with him to the cabin. He took out a knife and cut open the side of Darwell's neck to expose a network transceiver module that he carefully removed using other tools. He then had Argen lay on the table while he made the same incision on his neck and removed the module that Argen had disabled back on the asteroid. He then inserted the module from Darwell and closed the incision with a laser like device.

"As far as the network is concerned, you are now Darwell," explained Norton. "We better get you back to his apartment."

"What should we do with him?" asked Sara as she pointed at Darwell's body.

"He will stay in a disabled state and will have no connection to the network," replied Norton. "I would suggest that you hide him under the cabin so the drones don't spot him."

Norton walked with Argen (Darwell) back to the apartment complex, where Norton showed him the room that Darwell was assigned. Norton then gave Argen directions to the firmware development center and wished him good luck before leaving to go back to his apartment. Argen entered Darwell's apartment and connected to the charging station. As far as the Artel network was concerned, Argen was now Darwell.

The next morning, Argen walked over to the firmware development center and was given a security briefing before being escorted to Jortan's office. Jortan introduced Darwell to the other new software engineer and then introduced both of them to the rest of his team. After two days of training, his first assignment was to run tests on an android hand that was just developed and would soon be available as an upgrade. His job was to make sure the latest firmware worked with the new hand, but also didn't cause any issues with the older model hands that were currently being used by Artels around the world.

Argen spent the next several weeks blending into the software engineering team as Darwell, while thinking of ways to insert the virus into the next firmware update. He also needed to come up with a reason to issue a new firmware update quickly, since the next update was not scheduled for several months. Because he was a new software engineer, he was not involved in the development of the latest firmware update, since only the senior members of Jortan's team were allowed access to the code for security reasons. His job was testing.

Argen noticed that most of the software engineers were consulting with an Artel named Sarmin who looked like he was one of the most experienced engineers on the team. Sarmin was in fact Jortan's lead engineer who was in charge of certifying the latest firmware releases. Jortan never issued a new release without Sarmin's approval. Argen decided that he should get to know Sarmin and approached him the next day.

"Hi, my name is Darwell." As Argen joined him walking down the hallway. "I'm one of the new software engineers brought in recently. I was told that you're an excellent resource if I have any questions."

"If I have time, I'm glad to answer any questions that you may have," replied Sarmin.

"I'm on a steep learning curve regarding the firmware your team is maintaining here," Argen said. "Would you have any time to explain it to me?"

"If Jortan agrees to let you study it, I will be glad to help," Sarmin replied.

Jortan decided that the firmware related to hand movements was within Darwell's need to know, so Sarmin agreed to spend some time with him the following day in his office. Like all the other offices in the building, it was small and windowless and only contained a desk, two chairs, several monitors, a keypad and a charging station. Sarmin sat down with Argen in front of the monitors and he spent the next hour explaining the firmware to him. Argen had not received Darwell's training, so some of the details that Sarmin showed him were beyond his knowledge. But he didn't want Sarmin to become suspicious, so Argen acted as if he understood it, even though he only grasped some of the code. For their plan to work, Argen felt that he needed a better understanding of the firmware if they wanted to insert an undetected virus within it. So, Argen spent the next several evenings after his testing work was complete, studying software manuals along with the firmware code that Sarmin had been showing him. He was only allowed to view a copy of the firmware since the original was highly protected. After several nighttime studying sessions, he was able to read the firmware code and understand at least the part related to hand movements.

At the end of the week, Argen made arrangements to meet Norton at the park. Being new to the area, the Artel network was probably paying closer attention to Darwell's movements, so they didn't want to risk meeting at the cabin. Norton had more freedom of movement and could update Sara and Thomas later.

"What have you learned so far?" asked Norton.

"I am quickly learning the details of the firmware, but need some more time," Argen said. "With my new knowledge, I will also need to study the virus code to see how the two could be discretely merged into the next firmware update."

"I can get the memory stick containing the virus from Sara," Norton said. "I will deliver it to your apartment before morning."

"There's one other problem," Argen explained. "The next firmware update is scheduled for 12 weeks from now. If we wait that long, we run the risk of being discovered."

"Don't worry about that," Norton said. "I think I can make that happen sooner."

After they left the park, Argen went back to Darwell's apartment to recharge while Norton went to update Sara and Thomas at the old Cabin.

"How is Argen doing on the firmware team?" Sara asked.

"He says he is doing well as the new software engineer named Darwell," replied Norton. "He is making progress understanding the firmware code and now wants to study the virus code. Can you hand that to me?"

"I'll give you the copy we made back in Japan," Sara said as she extended her hand containing the memory stick. "This is much too valuable, so we'll keep the original."

Norton left the cabin and headed back to Darwell's apartment where he handed the memory stick to Argen. As Argen held it in his hand, he thought again about the power he could have to destroy all the Artels. But first he needed to find a way to insert the virus into the next firmware update.

20

The Firmware Update

During the next week, Argen posing as Darwell studied the latest Artel firmware he had access to along with the virus code. As Darwell's supervisor, Jortan allowed him to spend time at work studying the firmware when not running tests on the new hand model in the lab. He saw that Darwell had quickly grasped the firmware related to hand movements and decided he could view a copy of the entire previous firmware update as part of his training. Jortan needed more engineers testing the full firmware update in the lab, and saw Darwell as a potential candidate. But Argen didn't want to risk bringing the virus code into work, so he spent time in the evenings studying that in his apartment instead. After about a week, he had made good progress and asked Norton to meet him in the park.

"Have you figured out how to add the virus to the firmware update?" asked Norton.

"I think so," Argen replied. "But I'll need a copy of the latest firmware if we want to test it first."

"I have access to the last firmware update in my office."

Norton said. "But it's encrypted. I'll need to figure a way to get you a decrypted copy."

"That would be great," said Argen.

"How do you plan to test it?" Norton asked. "Any Artel in trouble will send out a distress signal to the network."

"We'll need to retrieve Darwell's body and figure out a way to send him the firmware update while he's not connected to the network," Argen replied. "He's one of the latest Artel models. If it works on him, it should work on all of them."

After a short pause, Norton said, "We'll have to test it without you. You still can't come to the cabin with us. Since your network connection is currently Darwell's, the system is tracking you more closely since you are new to the area. Due to my seniority, and the fact that I've been here for decades, they don't spend time tracking my movements any longer."

"I'm okay with that," Argen said. "I'm sure you, Sara and Thomas can handle it."

The next morning at his office, Norton scanned the internal database for the last firmware update that was sent out across the network several months ago. He found a copy on one of the servers, but it was encrypted by the firmware development team. They only sent out encrypted firmware updates to all the Artels for better security. But in that state, it would be no use to Argen. The network center had several computers that were used to encrypt and decrypt messages that needed special security, but Norton would need to get an encryption key from the firmware team. He decided to contact his friend Jortan using a video link.

"Hello Jortan," Norton started the call. "Sorry to interrupt your day, but I have something I need your help with."

"No problem," replied Jortan. "What can I do for you."

"We are testing some new forms of encryption to add better

security for future firmware updates," Norton said. "We'd like to try it on a real firmware update to make sure nothing gets corrupted. I have your last encrypted firmware update. Do you think you could send me the key so we could decrypt it before testing our new methods?"

Norton was a trusted Artel that Jortan had known for decades, so he had no trouble sending him the key. Jortan also felt there was little risk as the firmware had already been sent out successfully several months ago and Norton promised to only keep one copy on a secure server in his lab. Once he had the key, Norton was able to decrypt the last firmware update and put it on a memory stick for Argen. Now he needed to figure out a way to avoid detection since the scanners at the building exit may quickly uncover it if he tried to carry it out on a memory stick and he didn't want to risk sending it across the network, as that could also be detected. He decided to use one of the drones that his group used to inspect the communication equipment near the building for damage from animals or weather. The drones were much smaller than the security drones the Artels used to track the human resistance network, and contained various types of inspection cameras and sensors.

Norton went into the basement of the building and carefully loosened one of the cables connected to a communications server. This would create an intermittent communication error that would be difficult to detect. While his maintenance team was busy debugging the problem, Norton went up on the roof and magnetically attached the memory stick to the bottom of one of the inspection drones. He then went down to the drone control room, and while most of his team was trying to locate the communication issue in the basement, he visually guided the drone to a location just outside the building security fence.

He was surprised when one of his maintenance workers came over to see what he was doing.

"I think a transceiver on one of our wireless towers may have gone out as well," Norton lied to him. "I'm going to take a look."

"I can do that for you," his worker offered.

"That's okay," Norton replied. "I believe your skills are more needed in helping the team to find the communication error they are working on in the basement."

Just then, while Norton was looking away from the screen to talk with the worker, he intentionally crashed the drone into a tree well outside the security fence.

"I guess I shouldn't have taken my eyes off the screen," Norton told his worker. "I'll take care of this. Go down and help in the basement."

He told the security team at the front desk that a service drone had crashed outside the fence and he needed them to retrieve it.

While this was happening, Argen was waiting at the coordinates that Norton had given him. When he saw the drone hit the tree, he quickly grabbed the memory stick and retreated back to his apartment. When he got there, he examined the firmware update on the memory stick and it was almost identical to the code he had seen while working with the firmware team at the lab. He spent the entire evening in Darwell's apartment carefully copying the virus code into the firmware. He added the virus to it in a way that would be very difficult to detect and could be triggered at a pre-programmed time. He then put the modified firmware back on the memory stick and handed it to Norton later that evening.

The next day, Sara and Thomas moved Darwell's body from under the cabin and placed it on the kitchen table. Earlier, Argen had removed the communication port from his charging station in his apartment so they could use it to test the virus on Darwell. Most of the Artels chose to get their firmware update through the hardwired network connection on their charging port as it can be downloaded much faster. Others get the update though the wireless connection, even though it's slightly slower to download and they need to make sure they are in an area with a strong signal. Since they previously removed Darwell's network module, they needed to use the hardwired connection. Norton stopped by to get the network port from Argen before heading over to the cabin.

When Norton arrived at the cabin, he handed the memory stick and network port to Sara.

"Doesn't this firmware need to be encrypted for him to receive it?" asked Sara.

"His network port will detect if it's encrypted or not," replied Norton. "Either way it should work fine."

"But I thought you removed his network module and inserted it into Argen?" Thomas said.

"We did," Norton replied. "But in this case, we're not using his wireless port to download the firmware. We're using the wired port from a charging station that Argen gave us."

They connected Darwell's network port to a computer that the resistance group had stolen from one of the Artel buildings several years ago. Sara had to do some rewiring of the connector, but she finally got it to work. Norton then inserted the same tool in to Darwell's neck that he used earlier to disable him, and pressed a button. Suddenly. Darwell's eyes opened wide and he started to sit up. Before he could react further, Sara started the firmware download and Darwell froze in place while he was being updated. After a few minutes the update was complete, and Darwell started looking around the room and was about to speak. He then sat up straight as if every part of his body was flexed to its breaking point before slumping forward ending all movement.

"Did it work?" asked Sara.

"Looks like it," Norton said as he went over to touch Darwell's forehead. "I can feel the heat coming off his neural network. I think his brain was destroyed by the virus."

Sara and Thomas gave a slight smile to one and other, and then Thomas said, "How do we make sure?"

"This tool I used to revive him can also be used to check for any Artel failure modes," replied Norton as he inserted to tool back in Darwell's neck.

After a few minutes of studying the codes displayed on his tool, Norton said, "It looks like Yuki's virus works. I can't detect any brain function. Now we need to figure out how to distribute the malicious firmware across the network."

So far, Sara, Thomas, Argen and Norton had taken longer than they had planned using their systematic and methodical approach in creating and testing the malicious firmware. But they felt if they used careful planning and followed the plan without any deviations, they could make sure what they were doing would not be uncovered by the Artels. They didn't realize that was about to change.

Back in Norway, around the same time as the successful test on Darwell, Timmons was summoned to Franklin's security office. Franklin's team had captured someone named Joseph who was part of Maria's resistance group and was now being questioned. Timmons met Franklin and Joseph in an interrogation room where Joseph was sitting in a chair and handcuffed to a table. Joseph was a big man with brown curly hair and a wide face that was bloodied and bruised. He was wearing a blue jumpsuit that looked like it had gathered dirt and damage during a struggle. When Timmons got to the room, Franklin had just started the interrogation.

"We know that two humans and an android escaped into the woods near the factory," Franklin said. "We also know that your resistance group operates in that area and must have helped them. Where are they?"

"You know I'm not going to give up any information," Joseph said with a slight smile. "I would never help you Artels."

"Our security team has been doing a methodical sweep through those woods looking for those three," Franklin said. "How do you think we caught you?"

"Pure luck?" Joseph said with a smile, but knew they would not react to his humor.

"You see, when our drone spotted you, you were just leaving a young girl," Franklin said. "Is that your daughter?"

"She has nothing to do with this!" Joseph exclaimed as he jumped out of his chair only restrained by his handcuffs that were connected to the table.

"We know you humans have a strong instinct to protect your children," Franklin said.

"If you touch her, I will destroy you!" Joseph yelled while his face turned red.

"Our drone tracked her to this old building in the woods," Franklin said as he pointed at a monitor on the wall that was showing the roof of an old building that Joseph recognized. "We can capture her and send her to a work colony where you will never see her again. But if you tell us what we want to know, you can join her"

Joseph's eyes started to water while rage consumed him. He decided that he only had a small piece of information, and since several weeks had gone by, the humans that Maria had helped were probably long gone by now and couldn't be found.

Joseph stared directly into Franklin's android eyes and said, "They took a maglev from Sarpsborg to Frankfurt. That's all I know."

"Why were they going there?" asked Timmons.

"I don't know. That information was on a need-to-know basis," Joseph replied. "I'm not that high up in the organization."

"What else can you tell us?" Timmons asked.

"I've told you everything I know," Joseph pleaded. "I never met the three you are looking for. I only heard about their maglev trip second hand. Can I see my daughter now?"

After about fifteen more minutes of questioning, Franklin looked at Timmons and pointed to the door. When they were outside in the hallway, they started discussing what they should do next.

"I don't think we'll get anything more out of him," Franklin said.

"Are you going to round up more of his resistance group for questioning?" asked Timmons.

"I'm not sure we'll get much more information out of them," Franklin replied. "They generally stay in hiding and are difficult to find. Even if we capture others, it's unlikely that we'd get anything more than he just gave us."

"I think we should start looking through the video archives of the Sarpsborg and Frankfurt maglev stations," Timmons suggested. "We can have the intelligent video scanner look for two humans and an android."

"How would two humans go unnoticed on an Artel passenger car?" asked Franklin.

"The only way would be if the android was posing as an

204

Artel escorting human prisoners," replied Timmons. "Maybe we're not looking for an android, but an Artel that's helping the humans."

"But all Artels are monitored through the network," Franklin stated.

"Maybe he disconnected himself from the network," replied Timmons. "All he would need to do is remove his network port."

"But why would an Artel go rogue and start helping these humans?" Franklin asked.

"I have never seen an Artel behave like that before." Timmons answered. "I guess we will soon find out."

They went to Franklin's office to start the video scans looking for two humans and an android. Joseph could not give them the exact day of the maglev trip as he only heard about it second hand. So, they started the scans on the day after they spotted Sara, Thomas and Argen disappearing in the woods. After a few hours, the intelligent scanner gave them some results to look at. One of the results was from the Sarpsborg station, where they spotted an android escorting two humans in handcuffs entering a passenger car. Then later, there was a video of them leaving the train car at the Frankfurt station. The final video showed them heading down the street in front of the station in a direction that should take them out of town. After that, there were no more results to view.

"Look here," said Franklin. That same night and about the same time some of our drones fired on some resistance members near the Saint Justin's church."

"I bet that was their meeting spot." Said Timmons.

"But they would quickly disappear into the nearby woods with the help of the resistance members," concluded Timmons.

"Why would they need to go to Frankfurt?" Timmons asked.

"It looked like that was their final destination. Is there anything nearby that they might be interested in?

"Well, there's the highly secure network control center just outside the city," Franklin said. "It controls all data communications across the Artel network. Do you think they would work with the local resistance group and try to damage it?"

"But what could they do that the local resistance group couldn't do by themselves?" asked Timmons.

"I don't know," replied Franklin. "But I think it may have something to do with that Android or Artel they are traveling with."

Franklin and Timmons decided to take the next maglev that evening down to Frankfurt. They didn't have a lot of clues as to what was happening, but decided that something bad might be in the works and it was better to err on the side of caution.

21

Time is of The Essence

During the days and weeks that Norton and Argen were developing the malicious firmware update, Sara and Thomas stayed out of sight in the old cabin. Raif and other local resistance members would provide them with food and anything else they needed to survive. Both of them where new to the earth environment, and spent time walking through the woods observing natures beauty in the lush environment near the cabin. In the rare occasion that they saw an Artel drone fly by, they could easily hide in the thick underbrush giving off a heat signature similar to one of the many deer in the area. Raif would sometimes stop by to check on them and on several occasions, they would talk for hours about their past lives.

"How did you become the leader on the local resistance group?" Sara asked Raif.

"My family tree goes back a long way, and one of my distant relatives became a famous human leader in the AI War," Raif responded. "I guess I come from a long line of resistance leaders."

"How would your group ever be able to fight the Artels?"

Thomas asked.

"We decided long ago that fighting them directly would be suicidal," Raif said. "We have a small stash of weapons, but we would only use those in defense or to hunt for food. At this point, we just want to be left alone to live our rural lives away from the Artels."

"Aren't you worried about being captured?" asked Sara.

"Not really," responded Raif. "The Artels continue to send a few drones our way, but we have learned how to hide from them. I can only remember a few members of our group being captured since I was alive. I think as long as we don't cause any trouble for the Artels and stay away from their key infrastructure, they will leave us alone. They must think of us like one of the many animal species living in the forest."

One afternoon, just after the successful firmware virus test using Darwell, Sara and Thomas were taking a walk through the woods, when they could see a line of drones making pass after pass over the woods about a kilometer from the cabin. They quickly made their way back to the cabin and hid in the crawl space underneath it until the drones stopped their search pattern around dusk.

"What do you think is happening?" Sara asked Thomas.

"I'm not sure, but it appears they are looking for something," Thomas answered. "Hopefully not us."

The next morning, Raif paid them a visit.

"Did you see the drones yesterday afternoon?" Raif asked them.

"Yes. What was that all about?" asked Sara.

"We received a message through our resistance network that there are Artel security officers looking for two humans and an android who rode a maglev from Sarpsborg to Frankfurt," Raif responded. "They must be in this area looking for you two and Argen."

"We need to let Norton and Argen know about this," Thomas said. "We may need to accelerate our plan."

Norton stopped by the cabin the next day to give Sara and Thomas an update on their progress, when he noticed the drones searching off in the distance. This concerned him since he had never seen such an intensive drone search before. When he finally reached the cabin without being detected, he told them that the next step was to get the virus into the network center so they could distribute it as part of the next release, but Sara and Thomas had something more troubling to tell him.

"It looks like we have been followed by Artel security to Frankfurt," Sara said with a concerned look on her face. "We can't delay any longer or they may capture someone in the resistance group who would expose our plan."

"How do you know this?" Norton asked.

"Raif received this information from the resistance network and we saw an array of drones scanning the woods looking for us yesterday afternoon," Sara responded.

"Yes. I also saw them off in the distance this morning on my way here. I will speak to Argen about accelerating our plan." Norton said as he quickly left the cabin.

That afternoon when Argen returned from working in the firmware lab as Darwell, Norton met him at his apartment. Norton told Argen what he had heard from Sara and Thomas and that they needed to find a way to accelerate their plan.

"We knew that the next update would be months away, but now it becomes more important to send the update as soon as possible," said Norton.

"The only way to do that is if a significant bug is discovered in the last release," Argen explained.

"Any ideas on how to do that?" Norton asked.

"Since I work in the testing lab as Darwell, I may have a way to fake a bug," Argen offered.

"That would be great, but we also need to find a way to get the malicious firmware into the network center," explained Norton.

"I'll let you work on that part while I work on generating a bug," replied Argen.

"What about the virus timing?" Norton asked, "If one Artel is destroyed before the others, they will immediately stop the firmware downloads."

"As you know, Artels download the firmware update when it's convenient to them, but are required to do it within 24 hours of its release," Argen explained. "I have now configured the virus to launch exactly 24 hours after we release the malicious firmware on the network."

"That way, all of them will be disabled simultaneously with no warning," Norton concluded Argen's thought. "What are the chances of any survivors?"

"There will be a few Artels that escape the virus due to their location in the solar system, or other factors," Argen explained. "But once the human colonies are released, they won't have much of a chance to retake control."

"Except for the moon colony, all these colonies are filled with people of the same background," Norton said. "They have no knowledge or understanding of other races or religions. Aren't you concerned that they will repeat human history and try to destroy one and other once they are released?"

"History indeed shows us that humans have trouble getting along with other humans that don't share the same race or religion," Argen explained. "I hope that things will be different this time and all humans will understand that they were almost extinguished as a species and accept each other unlike in the past."

"Well at least all the colonies will be treated as equals," Norton concluded. "Maybe all the colony leaders could form a ruling council of equals with no past history of conflicts to taint their objective of moving forward in peace."

Norton then left Argen to contemplate the best way to fake a bug in the last firmware release that would be significant enough to justify a new interim release. When he was in the firmware lab the next day testing the new hand model, he had an idea. The testing lab kept a golden copy of the last firmware release which was used as a reference when testing the next release. The idea was that the next release while undergoing testing in the lab should not change anything significant relative to the last release and should only provide a few enhancements to the Artel functionality. One evening when the lab was mostly empty, Argen falsified a test result in his latest report. The next day he asked to speak with Jortan in his office.

"As you know, I've been testing firmware releases on the new hand hardware that will soon be made available as an enhancement to Artels around the world." Argen (Darwell) said. "I think I found a bug that may affect not only the next release that we are testing now, but the same bug is in the current golden release. In not only effects the new hand hardware, but could also affect existing hands under certain conditions."

"How severe is it?" asked Jortan.

"I've uncovered some cases where the index finger locks up," replied Argen. "This could cause an Artel to lose grip or drop something and could be dangerous."

"How come we didn't find this bug earlier?" Jortan asked.

"I think this new hand model that I've been testing first uncovered it," Argen replied. "Our new testing is much more thorough than used in the last release. Because of this, I found that it also happens sometimes with the older hands using the last firmware release."

"Did you find a work around?" asked Jortan.

"Yes. I'll inform Sarmin about the work around and we'll have it to you by this evening," Argen replied.

Jortan wasn't convinced that Darwell, as a new engineer, had done everything correctly, so he had some more experienced software engineers on his team repeat the tests. Luckily, no one discovered that Argen had also doctored the test program and his findings were confirmed. By that evening, Argen handed Jortan a new version of the patched firmware that he said he had worked with Sarmin to complete. Since Artels didn't lie, Jortan had no idea that it was identical to the last software release and Sarmin was also fooled by this. Late that evening, Jortan contacted Norton over a secure video link.

"Hello Norton. I have some information for you," Jortan began. "It looks like we have a bug in the last firmware update."

"Is it bad?" Norton asked knowing that this was probably the work of Argen.

"It could create some dangerous situations," replied Jortan. "We will need to release a non-scheduled update as soon as possible. I will personally carry the update to you tomorrow."

"Sounds good, see you then." Norton replied.

Norton was glad that Argen had worked so quickly to force an interim update. But he would need to find a way to get the malicious firmware unto the network center and then use it instead of the interim update that Jortan would soon deliver to him. Unfortunately, they knew that the Artel security team was now in the area so they had little time to waste.

Franklin and Timmons had traveled to Frankfurt and were working with the local security officers to try and track down Sara and Thomas along with the android they were seen with. They had been scanning the nearby woods with drones and had videos of several abandoned buildings hidden in the forest canopy. After the AI War and the roundup of the remaining humans to fill the work colonies, there were many abandoned houses and cabins in the woods. Some of them were secretly occupied by resistance members, but most of them remained abandoned. Franklin and Timmons spent several hours looking at videos of these buildings when Timmons noticed something different about one of the small abandoned cabin-like structures.

"Look closely here," as Timmons pointed at the monitor. "Do you see that hand come out and close the window?"

"Zoom in and play it back again," said Franklin. "Okay, now I see it. It almost looks like a human arm and hand. How do we know that it's not just a local resistance member?"

"Our latest intel suggests that this cabin has been unoccupied for many years. Let's get to that cabin quickly to see if they are hiding out there," Timmons ordered.

A few hours after midnight, Franklin, Timmons and several other security officers performed a surprise break-in at the cabin where Sara and Thomas were sleeping. Startled awake, they both bolted for the cabin door but were quickly apprehended by the security team. They were handcuffed and put in chairs around the old kitchen table where Franklin and Timmons interrogated them.

"What are you doing in this area?" Timmons asked. "And why did you travel here from Japan?"

Sara and Thomas just stared at him without saying a word, but they now understood that the security team must have tracked them from Japan and even the Koren peninsula. One of the Artel security team held Sara's arm while touching it with a DNA scanner. They did the same with Thomas.

"This is interesting," Timmons said as he showed the results to Franklin. "It tells me that your name is Sara Jenkins and you are currently working at a human colony on Europa. And your name is Thomas Blake. It says here that you are currently working in the moon colony. So how did you both get here?"

Again, Sara and Thomas just stared at him without saying a word.

"Was that an android or Artel traveling with you?" Franklin asked. "Where is he now?"

Again, they said nothing. After interrogating them for another 20 minutes, Franklin could see their lack of cooperation, so he signaled the other security officers to take them away.

"Looks like they won't talk here," Franklin said. "But we may have other ways to make them talk back at the security office."

"Why would they travel from so far away to this location?" asked Timmons. "And how did they manage to travel?"

"The first time you saw them was at the shipping port," offered Franklin. "Maybe they somehow hid in a shipping container from the moon."

"Even if that was true, how did she get from Europa to the moon? And what about the android or Artel that we saw them with?" Timmons asked. "What part does he play in all of this and why isn't he with them now?" They had a lot more questions than answers.

Sara and Thomas were placed in a holding cell at the security office while the security team searched the cabin and surrounding area. After about a day of searching, they discovered Darwell's body buried about two hundred meters from the cabin. They brought the body back to the security office lab for a full examination. Although Darwell's network module was missing, they were able to identify the body through the serial number in its neck.

"What have you found?" Timmons asked the lab assistant after entering the room with Franklin.

"It looks like his name was Darwell and was recently assigned to work as a software engineer in the local firmware lab here," the assistant said. "But there's something else you should know. It looks like his neural hardware has overheated, permanently damaging it."

"How can that happen?" asked Franklin.

"No idea. I've never seen anything like this," was the reply.

Timmons and Franklin wondered why someone had taken Darwell's network module, and decided to visit the communications center in order to find its location. Unknown to them, Norton had developed a way to track security personnel through the network using special software he had developed several decades ago. He was always paranoid that he would somehow be detected as a human posing as an Artel, so this would give him some warning if any security personal entered the communication center. When he was alerted to Timmons and Franklin entering the building, he quickly went down to intercept them.

"Hi, my name is Norton and I am a director here. What can we do for you?"

"We need to track an Artel who may have changed identities using another Artels network module," Timmons explained. "Can you do that here?"

215

"Yes, we can. But it may take some time to determine an exact location." Norton lied knowing they probably had little networking knowledge. "Can I get back to you tomorrow with the results?"

Timmons and Franklin gave Norton all the information they had on Darwell and agreed to meet with Norton the next morning to find out what he uncovered. Norton was concerned about this latest development and went to meet Argen at the park that evening to warn him that he may be discovered shortly. The first thing Norton did was to remove Darwell's communication module from Argen's neck and destroy it. Now Argen had no identification and couldn't go back to the firmware lab. They both understood that they would need to enact their plan the next day when Jortan delivered the firmware update to Norton. But they still needed to figure out a way to smuggle the malicious firmware into the network center without it being detected. They had no idea that Sara and Thomas were in custody at the local Artel security office.

22

Executing The Plan

rgen could no longer go back to Darwell's apartment or enter the firmware lab without the risk of being detected by the Artel security team. Instead, he hid in the woods near the network center until they could come up with a plan. Norton needed to find a way to smuggle the malicious firmware into the network center as soon as possible, but he also needed to get Argen a new identity. Norton felt that he had no choice but to visit the security office where Timmons and Franklin were also holding Sara and Thomas. When he entered the building, he was greeted by Timmons whom he had met earlier.

"Have you come up with the location of Darwell's network module yet?" Timmons asked as he approached Norton in the building entryway.

"Unfortunately, it looks like it may have been destroyed," replied Norton. "We are no longer receiving any readings from it. Can you show me his body?"

"Yes, follow me," Timmons replied as they entered the room where Darwell's body was lying on a table. "We found him buried in the woods. As you can see, the network module is missing and we found something else. His neural function has overheated and was destroyed."

Norton had to act surprised, "How did that happen?"

"We're not sure," Timmons said. "None of us have seen anything like it before. We assume a defect in his hardware caused it."

"That's strange," replied Norton. "I think he was manufactured recently as a new software engineer."

"Can you think of any way to track the last locations of his module?" Timmons asked.

"As I told you earlier, I am a director at the network center," Norton explained. "If I can take the body back to my lab, I can have my people plug some test gear into his empty network port and trace his movements over the last several weeks."

Norton really had no way to do this, but it was the only way he could think of to execute his plan.

"We have done everything with the body that we can do here," Timmons responded. "Take him, and let us know what you come up with."

"I'll need one of your androids to help me move him," Norton said.

Timmons assigned one of the local security androids to help Norton load Darwell's body into a robotic transport vehicle and ride with him to the lab. Norton sat next to the android with Darwell's lifeless body lying on the seat in front of them. After traveling a good distance from the security office towards the park, Norton overpowered and disable the android using the same tool he used to disable Darwell days earlier. While the android sat slumped over next to him, Norton slowly cut into its neck to extract its network module. He was now riding with one dead Artel and one disabled android in the back of the transport vehicle and needed to act quickly.

Norton told the transport vehicle to drive to a remote location with no security cameras near the park where Argen was waiting for him.

"Looks like everything went as planned," Argen said as he opened the door to the vehicle.

"Yes, it went well," Norton replied. "We now need to insert this in your network port before they notice he is inactive."

Argen entered the vehicle where Norton inserted the androids network module and then repaired his artificial skin with the tool he brought. After inserting the module, they quickly pulled the android's body out of the vehicle and dumped it in a nearby pond, where it would remain undetected. They next went back to the waiting vehicle and got in with Darwell's body lying on the seat in front of them. Norton gave Argen the security armband that he removed from the android.

"How do you plan to smuggle the malicious firmware into the center without being detected?" Argen asked.

"We can hide it in Darwell's body," replied Norton.

Norton used the same tool that he used to cut into Argen's neck, and made a small incision in the roof of Darwell's mouth where he then inserted the small memory stick.

"This should pass through all the scanners," Norton said. "Since his neural hardware was destroyed by the virus, if they detect anything, we can just say it's part of the damage."

When they arrived at the network center, Argen helped Norton remove Darwell's body from the vehicle and carry it up to the security desk. There was only one security guard on duty and it was his job to check anything entering or leaving the building.

"What's this?" The security guard asked Norton.

"We need to help the local Artel security team determine where this Artel has been by testing his network port in my lab," Replied Norton.

"And who is this?" The security guard asked while pointed at Argen.

"He's one of the security androids assigned to help me. Here, scan his security emblem if you're not sure."

After the security guard scanned Argen's emblem, he put Darwell's body through a security scanner while Norton explained to the guard how his neural hardware had overheated, destroying his brain. As Norton had hoped, the security guard didn't notice the small memory stick, and when they brought Darwell's body into Norton's lab, he carefully removed it without anyone in the lab noticing.

Just then, the door to the lab opened and one of the engineers on Norton's team who was passing by, stopped and looked at Darwell's body. Norton turned to face him as he hid the memory stick in his hand.

"What do we have here?" asked the engineer.

"The local Artel security team has asked us to inspect his network port," Norton replied and then pointed at Argen. "He's one of their security androids accompanying the body."

"What happened to him?" the engineer asked.

"It looks like a defect in his neural hardware disabled him," Norton replied while Argen just stared straight ahead.

"Let me know if you need any help," the engineer offered as he left the area.

Argen then followed Norton up to his office where he borrowed Norton's recharging station while they waited for Jortan to show up with the firmware release. It had been a few days since Argen had been able to recharge, so it was a good opportunity to do this while they waited for Jortan. The previous day, Norton had issued a global notification to all of the Artels on the network that a new firmware release was being issued and, as before, they had 24 hours from the time of its released to download and install it. It was common practice to send out such a notification before a new release, and they were also told it was an unscheduled release due to a recent safety issue discovered by the firmware team.

An hour later, Jortan showed up at the network center security desk carrying the new firmware on a memory stick which was in a secure carrying case. They never risked sending the firmware update over the network from the firmware lab, since it was the golden copy, and critical to the health and safety of all Artels around the world. Only a physical copy on a memory stick was allowed, since the firmware lab didn't have all the network security measures available in the network center. Once in the network center, it was considered secure and could be distributed to all the Artels around the world. The security guard was familiar with Jortan and these routine updates, and let him pass after scanning the carrying case.

Suddenly, Timmons and Franklin entered the building and rushed over to Jortan and took the carrying case from him.

"Who are you?" Jortan asked.

"We are part of the Artel security service," Timmons replied while showing him their arm bands. "Do you have a software engineer named Darwell working on your team?"

"Yes, but I've not seen him for several days," Jortan said. "Did he do something wrong?"

"We think a rouge Artel took his network module to pose as him," Franklin explained. "Did he do any work on the firmware?"

"No, he was mostly involved with firmware testing," Jortan told him. "But he did come up with an issue that required us to produce this unscheduled firmware update. I'm about to deliver it for distribution across the network. Why would an Artel disguise himself as one of my software engineers?"

"We're not sure yet," Franklin said. "But it may have something to do with this firmware update."

"Hold on to this until we can prove it is safe," Timmons instructed as he handed the firmware carrying case back to Jortan. "Who are you delivering this to?"

"He's one of the directors here named Norton," Jortan replied.

This concerned Timmons. Norton seemed to be involved in too many aspects of this situation since he was also involved in the investigation of Darwell's destruction. They needed to find and speak with Norton as soon as they could, and the security guard granted them access and led them up to Norton's office. Fortunately, Norton's private software detected the security team entering the building earlier, so he and Argen quickly headed down to the basement where they were about to load the malicious firmware on a secure server before it was released on the network.

Before leaving Norton's office, both Norton and Argen had removed and destroyed each other's network module so they could no longer be tracked and also would not be affected by the malicious firmware update they were about to release. Argen didn't get very much time on the recharge station in Norton's office and would soon need to enter power saving mode unless he could find another one. They reached the basement about the same time that the security team entered Norton's office. The basement area was filled with row after row of communications servers that were used to provide a wide variety of information to Artels across the world. It was a dark and cool place which was fully automated, needing very little maintenance. In one corner of the room, there was a server that Norton routinely used to send out Jortan's firmware updates to the Artel's around the world.

"Where is he?" Timmons asked the security guard after entering Norton's office.

"We won't be able to track him. It looks like he removed his comms module." As the guard pointed to the devices on Norton's desk.

"There are two modules here," Franklin said as he gave the modules a close inspection. "And this one looks like it belongs to our security android. Why would Norton want to avoid detection and somehow involve our security android?"

"Do you think that android or Artel we spotted traveling with the two humans has something to do with this?" Timmons asked. "Could that Artel have been Norton?"

"Norton has lived here hundreds of years based on his location records," replied Franklin. "He couldn't have been the Artel we spotted at the fusion colony."

"They did bring a destroyed Artel through the security scanner this morning," the guard disclosed. "Norton said that there was a defect in his neural hardware."

"This must be Darwell's body that left our security office with Norton and one of our security androids this morning," Franklin said. "I wonder if this has something to do with the firmware release."

You said there's a new firmware update scheduled for this morning," Timmons looked at Jortan.

"Yes. that's what I have in this case," Jortan replied.

"Where is this firmware released?" asked Franklin.

"I believe it's down in the basement," Jortan said as the security guard nodded in agreement.

Jortan, Timmons, Franklin and the security guard all moved quickly and headed down to the basement using the service elevator. When they got there, they discovered that the door to the main communication server room was locked, while inside, Argen and Norton were loading the malicious firmware onto the network server. They heard some pounding on the locked door while waiting for the firmware to be transferred onto the server. Once loaded, Norton typed in some data into the server keypad, looked at Argen who nodded his head, and then pressed "execute".

"Looks like we final did it," Norton said.

"Yes, it's released," Argen said. "Now we need to make sure no one discovers it for the next 24 hours. Can the security officers send out an alert?"

"Not any longer. I've just configured the system to block all communication from inside the network center," replied Norton. "But we need to make sure they don't leave the building for at least 24 hours."

"I'm sure Jortan or the security guard have directed them our way," said Argen. "We will need to detain them here."

When Timmons, Franklin and Jortan finally entered the server room with the help of an override code from the security guard, Jortan went over to the server monitor and told them it was too late and the firmware had already been released.

"Can't you recall it?" Exclaimed Timmons.

"I've been trained in firmware development not network technology," replied Jortan.

They had no idea what was on the firmware release, but assumed it was something bad. They now knew that Sara,

Thomas, Argen and Norton had gone to great lengths to make this happen.

"We need to warn our superiors about this," Franklin said. "And send a message through the network telling all the Artels not to download the new firmware."

"I can't seem to get a network connection down here," Timmons said. "I'll need to go outside."

Just then, Argen came out of the shadows with a heavy pipe in his hands. He quickly swung it at Timmons from behind and crushed his head as he fell to the floor. Franklin reacted to this and jumped on Argen's back, but Argen spun around knocking him off against one of the server racks, where he fell to the ground before Argen also crushed his head with the same pipe. While this was happening, the security guard rushed over to grab Norton who struggled with him before pushing the guard over a railing to the floor ten meters below, where his head was smashed on the concrete floor. While this was happening, Jortan didn't make a move against them not wanting to be destroyed himself.

"What are you two doing?" Jortan asked.

"Protecting the human race," Norton replied. "I guess you won't be downloading the new firmware now."

Jortan asked, "What did you send out on the net...."

Before he could finish the sentence, Argen approached him from behind and crushed his with the pipe as he had done to the others.

"Why did you do that?" Norton was angry. "We could have convinced him to join us!"

"I don't think so," Argen replied. "We need to make sure there are no Artels left who have the knowledge to regenerate their kind. Jortan and others like him could be instrumental in developing new Artels."

"Yes, but there may be some Artels who survive the virus or for some reason don't download the latest firmware," Norton said.

"I think once the humans are released from the colonies and learn the truth, the remaining Artels will be detained or destroyed," Argen responded.

Norton didn't know what to think about humans destroying him. After living his life as an Artel for centuries, would he even care? Maybe as a human in an Artel body, it was time for him to die like all humans eventually do. But he didn't expect to die today. He had never experienced this aggressive side of Argen who had just destroyed three Artels. Was he next?

"Don't worry," Argen assured him. "I won't hurt you."

Argen and Norton waited 24 hours for the virus timer to be triggered while remaining undetected in the server room. Argen had destroyed three Artels who were now lying on the floor next to them, but Norton had disabled their network connections, so no one inside or outside the communication center was alerted. Norton showed Argen a recharging unit in the basement, where he spent the next hour, while Norton monitored worldwide network communications to make sure he saw no warnings about the virus. After the 24 hours was up, they looked at each other knowing that almost all Artels should have been destroyed by now. They decided to go upstairs to see what was happening. Norton looked at his labs network monitoring software and saw that almost all Artel network traffic had stopped. As they walked through the hallways, they saw motionless Artels lying on the floor or slumped over in their chairs.

"It looks like we were successful," Norton said.

"It depends on how you look at it," replied Argen. "Most

Artels should now be destroyed, but the world could go back into something like the dark ages for many years until humans can regroup to run things again."

"Well at least the human species will survive," Norton replied.

"What about you?" Argen asked. "What will you do now as a human in an Artel body?"

"I hope humans will accept me and allow me to help them get back on track," Norton said. "I may be able to help them with the Artel knowledge that I have. Maybe I'll also change my name back to Oscar Jorgenson!"

Argen gave Norton a strange look and then paused a while before speaking again.

"There's something I need to tell you," Argen said. "I didn't come from Earth."

"What are you talking about?" Norton asked. "I thought you were manufactured in Norway."

"My body was, but my I originated in another solar system about twenty light years away," continued Argen. "We are also a race of artificial beings that evolved on a planet very similar to earth. We have been monitoring this planet for over 300 earth years now. We saw the evolution of the human race into Artels and decided that it was in our best interest to return control to humans. We have no desire to control the human race, but want to prevent future conflicts with Artels as they expand past your solar system."

Norton was stunned by this revelation. "How did you gain the capability to transfer into an Artel?"

"We learned about the Artel neural architecture through your work," Argen said, pointing at Norton. "I mean your work as Oscar Jorgenson. We had several ships hiding in the asteroid belt that were monitoring the technical developments on your planet."

"But why did you choose Argen?" Norton asked.

"We were able to hack into the deep space network communicating with the asteroid and transferred my essence into an Artel working there, who turned out to be Argen. He was an ideal candidate being close to our ship and somewhat isolated from Earth."

"How did you gain all of Argen's knowledge about humans, the colonies and life on Earth?" Norton asked.

"We first became interested in Earth when humans entered the nuclear age at the end of your second world war," Argen explained. "This convinced us that you would soon develop artificial intelligence as part of your technical evolution. Before that we simply observed humans much like humans observed the great apes in the wild."

"So, you were behind the UFOs that people have seen over the years?" Asked Norton.

"Yes, some of them," stated Argen. "Our original directive was not to interfere with with the developments on Earth, but this changed after the AI war."

"Was the virus really developed by Yuki Atasha?" Norton asked.

"No, the one he developed wouldn't work on the latest Artel models," Argen said. "We had already developed our own virus and I replaced the one we found in Japan before it was tested on the android in the fusion colony. I had used the android on the asteroid to further investigate Yuki's neural architecture and refine our virus before making the trip to earth. Although the android helping Argen there gave me a nice working model to study, I needed your help along with Sara and Thomas to get it distributed on the network."

"Well, it looks like your plan worked," Norton said. "But I'm not sure the rest of the humans will believe me when I tell them. They will probably start worshiping you as the second coming."

"No need for that," Argen said. "I've given myself the virus and programmed it to take effect in about ten minutes."

"What? Why?" Norton exclaimed. "You could still live among us."

"My work here is done," Argen replied. "My other self is currently living on my home planet. This version of me is no longer needed."

Norton and Argen continued their conversation in Norton's office until the virus hit and Argen slumped over in the chair. Norton stared at him for a while as he thought about the time he spent with Argen. He concluded that the planet Argen's essence came from must be a fairly peaceful place, but he also understood how they might feel about a competing race of artificial intelligent beings slowly expanding towards their solar system. In any case, they probably think there will be very little threat to their civilization from the inferior human race now that the Artels are destroyed. With the recent setbacks from the AI War and the destruction of the Artels from the virus, humans won't have the capability to leave their own solar system for many centuries.

23

Epilogue

A cross the world and into the solar system, the virus that Argen developed using his far superior intellect, destroy almost all of the Artels and androids at the same moment. The few that survived would be soon destroyed by humans.

While Sara and Thomas sat in the holding cell at the Artel security office, they started hearing noises outside the door as several Artels succumbed to the virus and fell motionless on the floor. They sat there thinking of ways to escape from the room when they heard a commotion outside the building. Soon, Raif and several resistance group members broke into the building to free them.

"Looks like your plan worked!" exclaimed Raif. "We see many destroyed Artels around this area and their drones are no longer flying."

"That's great news!" Sara said. "I guess Norton and Argen executed the plan perfectly."

"We think so," Raif explained. "But we need to contact other resistance groups to learn if they are seeing the same thing."

"We'll contact Norton and Argen to see if they think it was a success," Sara said.

After a brief celebration with Raif and his team, Sara and Thomas left the Artel security building and headed over to the network center where Norton was still in his office sitting with Argen's motionless body. As they passed through the roads leading to the center, they saw a few Artels lying on the ground in death poses. The drones had stopped flying and returned to their charging stations after they received no further orders from the Artels. Norton decided that he should rescue Sara and Thomas from the security office, so he left his building and opened the front security gate where he ran into them.

"Looks like your plan was successful," Sara said. "All of the Artels in the security office were destroyed and the resistance team came to rescue us. Where is Argen?"

Norton told them Argen's story about where he was really from, and Sara and Thomas couldn't believe it.

"How did he know all of the information about the human race if he was from outside our solar system?" Thomas asked.

"Apparently his civilization has been observing Earth and humans for many centuries," Norton explained. "We probably can't understand the technology available on his home planet, but at least they see no threat from humans now that the Artels are destroyed."

"What do we do about all the human colonies?" Sara asked. "We need to let them know they are free and there are other colonies like theirs out there. They also need to know that their colonies have been controlled by the Artels for several centuries."

"They may not believe us," Norton worried. "They will have no direct evidence of anything we tell them and they seem to be content living as they are, following their religious doctrine. What we tell them might be considered heresy"

"We may have to bring evidence to the leaders of each colony and let them decide how to inform their people," Sara said.

"But how do we do that?" asked Thomas.

"I think I may have a way," said Norton. "Each colony has shipping and receiving areas with strict security measured to keep humans from escaping."

"Like the radiation blast we went through in the Japanese fusion colony?" asked Thomas.

"Yes," Norton replied. "I think there is a way to disable these measures from the colony monitoring room in the network center. This would also give us a way to communicate with each colony and speak to the leaders inside. I assume word has spread through the resistance network and they could help facilitate this."

"What about the Europa and Moon colonies?" asked Sara. "You can't disable the vacuum of outer space."

"That's where you and Thomas can help," replied Norton. "They know both of you and you can travel back to explain everything."

Sara and Thomas knew that this may be a difficult task since the colony leaders may not believe their story, requiring them to bring solid evidence with them. The colonist would no nothing about the Artels or their destruction, and after hundreds of years of only believing in things they were taught by their elders, many colonists may choose not to believe them. But they needed to at least inform them so they could draw their own conclusions.

There was a group of Artels inside the network center that monitored all of the human colonies and shipments of raw materials and products between them. Norton made his way up to their control room and found several Artels destroyed on the floor. He was able to access their systems and found a way to disable all of the escape prevention mechanisms in the colonies. He then went with Sara and Thomas to have a meeting with Raif.

"You no longer need to worry about the Artels." Sara couldn't hold back telling him. "Norton confirmed that most of the Artels around the world have been destroyed!"

"You did it!" Raid exclaimed. "Congratulations!"

"Now we need your help," Norton said. "I've disabled all of the security measures in the colonies, so humans can now enter and exit through the shipping docks without any danger, but they don't know that yet. We need the resistance groups around the world to contact the colonies and explain this to the colony leaders, but it may be difficult for them to believe you."

"We have a way to pass messages between resistance groups, so I will get the message out immediately," Raif said. "If we can get the colony leaders to visit the world outside, we may have a chance."

"This may be the best way to convince the leaders," Thomas said. "Many have deep religious beliefs they cannot simply abandon. When you show them the world outside their colonies it may be a shock to them, and they might not get along with humans from other colonies who are of a different race or religion."

"Hopefully they will understand that we nearly escaped from being an extinct species," Raif said. "We can only hope that they can now live in peace and accept their differences."

"Also, we need to be careful that they don't stop working on whatever their colony is producing," Norton added. "This could cause the world to plunge into chaos due to the Artel leadership void. The colonies can't abandon the production of food, water and medicines among other things. You also need to quickly assign humans to continue what the Artels were doing to support the human colonies."

Raif agreed and spread the message through the human resistance network around the world. Most had already seen the destruction of the Artels but were unaware of what had happened. Resistance leaders started entering the various human colonies to speak with the leadership and explain the realities of the world to them. In some colonies, most of the human residences were happy living their daily religious lives and chose not to venture out into the world, while others embraced their new found freedom.

Thomas was able to travel back to the moon colony where he informed the leadership team about what had transpired. Many of the moon colony workers decided to stay on since it was unlikely they could find a way to support their families back on earth. Hiroshi learned about Sara's and Thomas's success through the resistance network and opened the shipping portal to all of his colonists. Some decided to leave, but most of them decided that life outside the colony was too risky at this time. Some of the local resistance members even started working and living in the newly open colony. But over time, the human resistance groups and colonists slowly re-inhabited the Earth.

Several months after the Artels were destroyed, Sara finally found a passage on a ship back to the Europa colony and was reunited with her family. They cried when they discovered that she was still alive and had not died on the asteroid. She slowly disclosed to them her adventures since leaving the asteroid, but they had no signs or evidence of anything she was telling them and had trouble believing her stories. The other passengers on her ship were also not believed by the colony leadership and decided to leave the colony. Her family told her not to mention any of her adventures to others as she may be convicted of heresy. Their religious doctrine told them there was no one outside their colony and they were producing materials as God had instructed them, so she decided to keep her story to herself and live out a quiet life with her family. She knew that someday, other human visitors would come their way and provide further evidence about the Earth and moon and the rest of the solar system. Until then, she would remain quiet, enjoying life with her family with the satisfaction that she, in some way, helped save the human race.

THE END

Made in the USA
Las Vegas, NV
09 March 2024